Jinx of the Black Lynx

Written and illustrated by
David Schmidt

Brule, Wisconsin

Jinx of the Black Lynx

First Edition

Published by:

Cable Publishing
14090 E Keinenen Rd
Brule, WI 54820

Website: www.cablepublishing.com
E-mail: nan@cablepublishing.com

Soft cover: ISBN 13: 978-1-934980-30-9
ISBN 10: 1-934980-30-7

Library of Congress Control Number: 2010930873

Printed in the United States of America

This book is dedicated to Sam –
for finding a diamond in the rough
and believing in me enough
to be not just my mentor,
but also my friend.
– DS

A butterfly gently fluttered over a peaceful meadow and landed on a small sapling. Its bright orange and yellow wings silently flapped as it tried to keep its balance on the thin twig.

Chirps from dozens of birds and the occasional chatter of insects were the only sounds that radiated from the quiet valley. A soft wind gingerly blew against the trees and mildly tossed their leaves about. The tall grasses and wildflowers on the forest floor slowly swayed back and forth like waves on the shore of a calm lake.

Suddenly, two small, furry animals burst from the tree line and tumbled in a heap out into the sun.

"Gotcha!" exclaimed the smaller of the two, a gray wolf pup. "Ya can't hide from me! I've got natural hunting and tracking skills!"

"Oh, gimme a break, Mesquite," said the other round ball of fur, a grizzly bear cub. "I stopped playing hide-and-seek when I came across those raspberry bushes. I was on a l-l-lunch break," he stuttered. The little bear liked to eat.

"Sequoia, you lost fair and square and now you're gonna have to find me!" Mesquite quipped.

"I'm tired of this game. Let's g-g-go mess with Aspen instead," the little grizzly offered.

"Okay, loser, since you can't win anyway." Mesquite snipped. "I think she's up on the bluffs. My mom said she saw her this morning."

The two friends started off across the valley toward a large, rocky summit overlooking the meadow.

"Why does she always want to g-g-go up there?" Sequoia asked.

"She likes to pretend she's flying since she's not very good at it," Mesquite said. "Her mom and dad get her up there and show her that peregrine falcons are good flyers and she should be soaring with them by now."

"M-m-maybe she's really not a peregrine falcon at all," Sequoia joked. "Maybe she's a chicken!"

Mesquite burst out laughing at the little bear's comment as they plowed headlong through the long grasses toward the path that led up the cliff.

After the duo had plodded along for nearly an hour, they finally neared the top of the bluff. They could see their little friend, Aspen, out on the edge of a craggy rock. She had her eyes closed and was holding her wings out, pretending to be soaring above the valley. The wind was blowing against her, rustling her feathers as though she was actually flying.

Mesquite hunkered down so she wouldn't see him. "Hey, Sequoia," he whispered to his friend, "let's sneak up on her and scare her off the cliff! We'll teach her to fly, all right!"

"Not me. You g-g-go ahead. She'll tell her mom and her

mom will tell my mom and I'll g-g-get grounded until hibernation time!" the bear replied.

"Fine. I'm not scared. You just sit back and watch an alpha-male wolf in action!" Mesquite said confidently.

He turned away from Sequoia and peered quietly over some blades of grass. He got ready to pounce.

Whack!

Without warning, a small white and blue wing slapped Mesquite across the face and he fell over backward, holding his nose with his front paws.

"Thought you could sneak up on me, huh?" Aspen said proudly, as she tucked her wing back alongside her body. "I heard you a mile away, you idiot!"

"It was his idea!" Mesquite said, pointing his paw at Sequoia.

"Oh, really!" Aspen said, glaring at the bear cub.

"N-n-no it wasn't!" Sequoia stammered. "It wasn't me. He's lying! Mesquite, I'm gonna kick your –"

Suddenly, the roar of a private jet cut off the adolescent grizzly. It cruised low and fast and blasted by them with a horrendous shudder. It was a stealthy, high-tech aircraft – shiny black in color, but with bright red symbols on the sides. It was making a high-speed getaway back to its home base after a secret and successful mission of arson.

"What was that?!" Aspen exclaimed. "How rude!"

The three friends shook the dust off and looked in the

direction of the jet. It was already out of sight.

Sequoia stuck his nose up and smelled the air in the jet's wake. "Do you smell smoke?" he asked.

Mesquite and Aspen joined their friend in sniffing the air. The normally fresh, clean air of the valley was mixing heavily with the scent of burning wood.

"You're right," Mesquite said. "The forest is on fire!"

The trio bounded over to the other side of the bluff from where the jet had first appeared for a better look at the valley below.

What they saw shocked them. A wild, ferocious fire was rapidly consuming the forest below. Orange and red flames ripped at the trees and grasses as clouds of thick, grayish-black smoke poured upward into the sky. The fire was accelerating and encircling the entire valley. It looked as though it would consume everything.

"We gotta get home!" the three friends exclaimed at practically the same time.

Aspen leaped off the cliff, flapping her little wings fiercely as she struggled to fly. "I'll check the way!" she yelled to the wolf and bear younglings as they hustled down the path to the valley below.

The artificially inspired fire raged and very quickly devoured everything in its path. It swarmed over the valley like a fiery flood.

In a panic, Mesquite and Sequoia scrambled down the trail. Terrified, they were trying to get back to their dens

where their families were surely waiting for them. As they rounded a corner near the end of the trail, they encountered Aspen on a tree limb overlooking the path.

"We can't go this way!" she shouted as she tried to catch her breath. Her wings were tired from flying just a short distance. "We have to go around to the east," she said, pointing with her wing. "If we can get over the river, we can catch up with our families from the other side. I won't be able to fly much more. We have to hurry!"

The boys nodded and headed off through the brush and around the hillside. It was slow going since there was no trail and neither of them had ever gone that way before. They were all scared.

The sky was blackening and all the smoke was blotting out the sun. It started to look like dusk even though it was a sunny afternoon. Everything had a dark orange, hazy look to it. The hoarse rumbling sounds of the fire made it hard to hear. The swirling winds generated by the flames carried an amazing amount of gray ash, making it look almost as if it were snowing.

The three animals finally got to the far side of the hill only to find the valley that faced them already submitting to the power of the flames.

"We've got to go back!" Mesquite shouted, and he started to turn around.

The fire was overrunning the forest behind them. Trees, still aflame, toppled in the forest and crashed to the

ground. The fire had surrounded them.

"There's only one way out!" Sequoia yelled above the noise and confusion. "We have to jump in the river and let it carry us out of here! Aspen, you can ride on me down the stream – I know you can't swim."

"Let's do it!" Mesquite plunged into the river and was immediately swept away by its torrent. Sequoia followed him in without hesitating. Aspen flew down and landed on the cub's back as Sequoia frantically tried to paddle for control.

The river rushed them along through the burning forest. They passed safely through intense patches of heat and thick black smoke. Flames leaped out from all directions but never touched the hapless trio as they whirled about in the rushing waters. Burning embers fell about them, extinguishing with a loud hiss as they hit the water.

After a while, the burning forest slowly disappeared behind them. The air grew cleaner and the sky was clearer as the river snaked its way down through a ravine.

The river was running faster and faster, and they soon found themselves at risk of being drowned instead of burned alive.

Mesquite and Sequoia were almost exhausted from swimming so hard. Aspen was doing all she could to hang on. Her little talons gripped the fur of her young grizzly friend as tightly as possible.

A short distance ahead, Mesquite could see the river becoming very rough, with jutting boulders and dangerous

fast-moving water. The drenched little wolf pup turned to his friends splashing violently behind him.

"We've got to get out of the river!" he shouted. "There's a dead tree up ahead hanging over the water. Grab onto it and pull yourselves out!"

The trio slammed into the fallen tree but managed to hang on with their claws as the rushing river pulled at them. Aspen had just enough energy left to fly onto the log and she shouted desperately for her friends to get out of the river.

Mesquite managed to get out first and, after getting a firm grip, he bent over and grabbed onto Sequoia with his teeth. He tugged and tugged until the soaked bear got a foothold on a branch and hoisted himself out of the raging waters.

They stumbled off the tree and collapsed onto a thin strip of ground. Panting heavily and trying to catch their breath, they could see that they were at the base of a rocky wall next to the river.

After a few minutes of lying there, trying to regain their strength, they were startled by a cry for help from the river. They bolted upright and peered over the river-bank. Swimming frantically just upstream, a small, lanky animal was helplessly heading for the rapids.

"W-w-we got to save her!" Sequoia bellowed. He sprang on the fallen tree and held his paw down into the water to try to rescue the distressed creature caught in the river's current.

As she came by, she latched onto the grizzly cub's thick paw. Sequoia lifted her easily out of the water and onto the relative safety of the tree limb. The wiry animal shook the water off herself and scampered to solid ground. The others could now clearly see that she was a young black-footed ferret.

"Oh, thank you, thank you. You saved my life!" she said to Sequoia as he joined them on the riverbank. "My name is Juniper. What's yours?"

The grizzly bear, gray wolf and peregrine falcon younglings introduced themselves to their new friend as wisps of smoke and ash swirled all around. The fire was darkening the sky above them. It was getting closer.

"C'mon," Mesquite said. "We've gotta keep moving. The wind's blowing the fire this way. We'll have to walk from here."

The exhausted quartet got to their feet and headed away from the approaching wildfire. The raging river was to one side of them, the rocky cliff to the other, and the fire was quickly approaching from the rear.

They didn't get more than a few dozen steps before their thin pathway stopped abruptly at the top of a sheer drop-off to the rapids below.

Aspen flew up onto Sequoia's shoulders to peer over the edge. "End of the road, guys," she said. "What are we going to do now?"

The animals looked around and at each other. Things had gotten pretty grim.

Just then, they heard a voice from the craggy rock face above. "Up here! Climb up! You'll be safe up here!" It was a badger cub calling down to them from a ledge.

The animals were relieved, but knew they couldn't scale the rocks to get to him.

"How do we get up there? It's too steep!" Juniper shouted up to him as she stood up on her back feet.

"There's sort of a path back that way a bit," the badger yelled down to them while pointing with his paw. "It's not easy, but you should be able to make it. You better hurry!"

The group wasted no time and a few minutes later, after clambering up the rocks, they came face to face with the little badger high above the river.

"C'mon," their rescuer said. "There's a cave back this way. We'll be safe there."

"Thanks, friend," Sequoia said. "What's y-y-your name?"

"Cedar," he said.

"Well, Cedar, I'm Sequoia," the bear said. "This is Aspen, that's Mesquite and she's Juniper."

"That's quite a wildfire," Cedar said as he glanced over his shoulder. "We should all consider ourselves lucky. Like you guys, I barely escaped getting cooked back there. Fortunately, I came across this cave."

The group walked around a large boulder at the mouth of the cave. Cedar led them into the cool, dark opening

and along a thin, sandy trail down deep inside the underground cavity. They eventually came to a larger open area where they all could sit and rest. In a few hours, the firestorm should harmlessly pass them by.

It took a moment for all of them to finally relax a little and dwell mournfully on the tragic events of the day. They were orphaned animals now.

Without warning, a man emerged out of the shadows of the cave. It was an elderly tribal chief. He wore a glorious headdress of feathers and beads. His clothes were made of buckskin, as were the moccasins on his feet. The old chief held a very old and oddly shaped walking stick. He made absolutely no sound when he moved and as he stepped forward, his feet never quite touched the ground. He seemed to be somewhat transparent.

The animals were startled by his presence. They jumped back and gathered tightly together on the other side of the cave.

"Do not be frightened," he said. "This is my home; I am the great chief of the shamans of the tribes of the four winds. You are my guests, and I have been expecting you for a very long time. You have been brought here to be together, for the five of you are truly one."

The badger decided that he had had enough of this stranger and his strange ways. He stepped forward a little and bared his teeth, hoping to scare the ghost-man away.

"I mean you no harm, Cedar," the Native American said. The ancient man could tell that they feared him.

Cedar backed down.

"Oh," the chief said as he chuckled a little. "I see you are shocked that I know your names. I know all of you and, believe it or not, all of you know me – at least in your hearts."

The animals looked at each other, puzzled. This was truly a day of amazing events.

"We speak the same language, you and I. Your ancestors taught us the ways of nature…the circle of life. They taught us to dance, to sing and to laugh. And they also taught us to fight and survive," the old spirit said. "And, now, it is time to fight again."

The tribal chief sat down, his legs crossed beneath him. He still did not touch the ground; instead he mysteriously hovered several inches above it.

"Gather around me, my brothers and sisters," the Native American said as he spread out his arms. "Much has been taken from you this day…but much is about to be given. You are a family now. Stay together, for you will be the law of the land."

The animals approached the spirit-chief, no longer afraid of him. They sat in a semicircle in front of him and listened intently.

The shaman waved his walking stick across the ground in front of them, and a small, bright-blue flame snaked up from under the sand and stones of the cave floor. It danced and flickered, finally growing into a small, mystical campfire. The flames generated no heat, only a metaphysical, turquoise-colored light that bounced off the

cave walls all around them.

"The earth has been dishonored too many times, my friends. She is bountiful, but she can take no more. The evil that has come over this land must be stopped. You five have been chosen to be her guardians," the elder revealed.

The animals heard ancient Native American drums and chants from invisible people echo throughout the cavern. The sounds grew louder and louder, but the old chief was the only one there with them. The blue-green blaze on the cave floor burned brighter.

"Now reach into the fire, my brothers and sisters. Remove a stone from the enchanted flames," he said.

The animals, eyes open wide in wonderment, hesitantly leaned into the magical blaze and each pulled out a small, flat stone. The strange turquoise fire did not burn at all, but tickled their skin. The five creatures of the forest sat back, looking down at the glowing gems in their grasp.

"Now turn them over, and you will see that each stone is marked with your imprint," said the spirit chief. The animals did as they were told and noticed their footprints had pressed into the rock on the other side.

"These are the source of your power; you must keep them with you at all times," he continued. "It is told that turquoise has healing and protective powers. It promotes spiritual harmony and dispels negative energy and impurity. You

have been granted great responsibility and great authority. The spirits of the entire first nations are behind you, and the fate of mother earth is before you."

The shaman reached into a satchel tied to his belt and pulled out five long, leather cords. He went to each animal, tied a cord to their amulet stones, and placed them around their necks like a pendant. He then stepped back behind the flickering fire and smiled at his animal audience.

"When you are in danger," he said as they looked up at him in amazement, "the amulets will bring the spirits of your animal and native warrior ancestors into your hearts. You will become more powerful than you can imagine. It is your destiny to right the wrongs of the land and bring balance back to the planet. You only have to believe...."

Suddenly, the blue-green fire separated into five distinct flames and shot straight into each animal's amulet. The necklaces glowed brightly with an intense neon-blue color that swirled about the five little animals like a tornado made of pure light.

Then, with one last powerfully brilliant flash, each animal transformed into his or her powerful, noble alter-ego. They raised up on their hind legs, human-like, in a proud, heroic stance with their heads held high and their chests jutting forward.

Mesquite transformed into a large, valiant humanoid

wolf with incredible fighting skills, armed with a long wooden staff with an enchanted spear tip that he could summon at will.

Aspen became a regal falcon-woman, her wings tipped with mystical feathers that she could shoot like missiles with deadly accuracy and power.

Sequoia morphed into a massive, muscular, fully grown man-like grizzly with a huge, unbreakable magical shield grasped in his left arm.

Cedar grew into a stocky, brawny man-sized badger with claws that could carve through steel and tunnel him at incredible speeds behind enemy lines.

Finally, Juniper changed into an ultra-athletic and extremely flexible ferret-woman blessed with super-speed. Whenever she transformed, a leather pack automatically appeared on her back that was filled with small wooden handles that she could magically turn into hatchets with just her touch.

The Natural Forces heroes looked at each other and felt their newly found power course through their superhuman bodies. Together, they felt unstoppable.

Without another word, the shaman chief had disappeared back into the shadows from which he came, bound for his home in the spirit realm.

Their adventures were about to begin and the world would never be the same.

NATURAL
FORCES
TM

The remote, deserted walking trail cut through the dense forest like a secret road known only to the area animals and the occasional humans who happened across it during a hike far away from the groomed and well-marked trails they normally traversed. Overhead, a thick canopy of leafy tree limbs filtered the sun's rays so well that the trail seemed to always be cool, wet and soft underfoot. Cushiony green expanses of moss – nature's carpet – covered much of the ancient pathway.

It was through this moist tunnel cutting deep through the massive timberland in northern Minnesota that five very special young animals found themselves meandering. It was a warm June morning.

"This place is amazing," the wolf pup in front named Mesquite said as he raised his snout in the air to breathe in an extra deep helping of the oxygen-thick, damp air. "I could live here forever!"

"Me too," his bear cub friend agreed. "There's w-w-water everywhere and I don't even have t-t-to work hard to find food!" Sequoia was an affable, portly little bear with a bit of a stuttering problem. He was the same age as Mesquite, but being a grizzly he out-weighed him by a good 25 pounds. They had been friends all their lives.

One of the five companions was a young peregrine falcon. She hadn't perfected the art of flying yet but still managed to flitter above the rest, going from branch to branch along the trail. She was named Aspen. "You know," she said loud enough for all to hear, "I'm surprised you're not sick to death, Sequoia. After drinking a whole quart of that green stuff you found in that human's cooler two hours ago, you should probably be puking your guts out by now."

"You don't know w-w-what you're talking about, Aspen," Sequoia retorted. "It was good! Sweet and c-c-cold and very yummy!"

"I think it was anti-freeze, you knucklehead," Aspen replied.

The little badger walking behind Sequoia piped in. "It wasn't anti-freeze," he said loudly. "I can read pretty good – it's some sort of lemonade the humans give to alligators."

Aspen squawked. "That's about the stupidest thing I've ever heard, Cedar! Why would people carry around bottles of alligator lemonade?"

"How am I supposed to know? I'm not a human. It's what was written on the bottle right over the orange lightning bolt symbol," Cedar, the badger cub, replied. He was getting annoyed. He was confident that he had read what was written on the label correctly.

"Well, whatever it was, Sequoia is doing just fine," the last member of the fivesome, a black-footed ferret called

Juniper, added. "If we find any more abandoned coolers, I want to try some. Unless they have ferret-ade! Do you think they make ferret-ade?" she asked hopefully.

"You're an idiot, Juniper," Mesquite turned back to say. "You're all idiots..."

The land they walked through tucked up against a large body of water known as Crane Lake on the southeastern side of Voyageurs National Park – a pristine Northwoods water wilderness preserve sandwiched between the Ontario Province in Canada and the western portion of Superior National Forest in the United States. It is truly a hearty landscape, lush with vegetation and brimming with animal and bird life alike. The lakes and rivers are filled with fish and swarmed by waterfowl.

People often frequent the park, in the summers mostly, when boaters, fishermen and vacationers delight in the remote vastness and cruise its waterways with canoes, kayaks and houseboats. Mosquitoes swarm the visiting humans and relish their annual visits to the territory.

The area is old and almost completely unchanged from the days when the native people of the Cree, Monsoni and Ojibwe tribes, many of whom still live nearby, inhabited the land. Clues remain to the presence as well of the trappers and fur traders from the north and east who came later to find fortune and fame in the watery peninsula.

This wilderness was set aside as a national park only a few decades ago and permanently halted the logging, mining and dam construction within its borders. It is now a clean, overwhelming natural expanse of thick woodland surrounded by seemingly endless miles of fresh water.

*****

Three thousand miles away, and twenty-five thousand feet up in the air, a shiny-black private jet airliner was cruising over the Atlantic Ocean, shuttling its occupants back to America.

The private aircraft belongs to the Axxes Conglomeration and on board was its president, Mr. Nathan Axxes himself.

Axxes is a power-hungry, greedy old man. He rules his mega-corporation with a ruthless, heartless attitude and will stop at nothing to keep his hunger fed.

A spindly character, he is tall and lanky with deeply set, soulless gray eyes and a long, silvery mane of hair. If vampires were real, Nathan Axxes would surely be suspect of being Dracula himself, if not a distant blood relative.

He was returning from a week-long trip to Africa where he was brokering a deal to double the number of children working in the largest diamond mine in the whole continent – owned by his company, of course. He had successfully destroyed any hopes the laborers had of improved

working conditions and reduced hours. Axxes is a brutal leader.

On board the executive jet, he was sitting comfortably in his calfskin-covered captain's chair. A crimson-colored crushed velvet curtain was pulled shut around him to offer some privacy. Axxes was reading through a stack of financial papers and slowly swirling the ice around in his drink with a long toothpick that was jabbed through a large green olive. The clinking of the frozen cubes against the antique crystal glass soothed his temperament somehow.

In addition to the pilots and a lone stewardess, a select few of his corporate aides were on board as well, mostly legal staffers and assistants. As usual, he was left alone, which is the way he prefers.

From the back of the plane, a phone rang. It was his private line.

The stewardess, a lovely lady of obvious Norwegian descent named Toni quickly answered it and brought the cordless phone over to her employer.

"Mr. Axxes, sir, you have a phone call," she nervously said as she stood beside his curtained suite.

A long-fingered and pale hand slithered out from behind the curtain. Toni placed the handset in it and scampered away toward the back of the plane.

"Hello, Miranda," Mr. Axxes said into the phone with his usual icy tone. He immediately knew who it was.

Miranda Wright is the Chief of Business Operations and his most powerful executive. She handles everything for him and covers up all of the corporation's illegal activities.

"Nathan, we have a problem," Miranda reported from the company's headquarters in Los Angeles. She was the only one who could call him by his first name, but never in front of others.

"Go on, I'm listening," Axxes replied.

"As you know, the robotic operatives and mainframe systems monitor all Internet activity across the globe and cross-reference key words and locations against our corporate ventures," Miranda relayed. "Well, we got a hit last night that concerns us."

Mr. Axxes was troubled. His grip on the phone tightened and his voice became graveled, "A hit. Where? What site?"

"Upper Minnesota," she said. There was a pause on the line. "The iron mine."

Nathan leaned forward in his chair. His temper was starting to flare and a hint of panic broke through his normally steely voice. "Miranda, you know what's in that mine. You know we have to protect it. Tell me exactly what we're dealing with here."

"We intercepted a message blog from some family of campers in a cabin not too far away from the site of the mine," she explained. "They mentioned in their web log that they were out hiking in the late afternoon when

their 12-year-old son spotted a lynx. A black lynx. And they are going out again tomorrow with a camera to try to get pictures of it."

Mr. Axxes was confused. "So? Who cares? A stupid wildcat is romping around the woods and we're concerned about it? Are you joking with me, Miranda? You know I hate jokes."

"Nathan," she went on, "I understand you have zero interest nor compassion for animals, so let me explain the impact this little sighting has on your little secret hidden away in that iron-ore mine up there. Allow me to explain and you'll understand why you pay me so much…

"You see, there is no such thing as a black lynx, Nathan. If this sighting of theirs is true, and especially if those idiots go back there and get pictures of the thing, then this little family just uncovered a new species. And if word gets out that a never-before-seen animal is around, then the Environmental Protection Agency, the Department of Wildlife and Natural Resources, all the media outlets and every tree-hugging, whale-worshipping member of the Sierra Club is going to be climbing over every inch of that land and looking in every nook and cranny in the entire forest to confirm their existence. And if they can do that, you can kiss your mine and its entire contents goodbye forever. And I'll be busy trying to keep you out of federal prison or put on trial for treason."

Axxes inhaled sharply, clearly startled and upset by

the prospect. A long delay hung on the line. Then he finally spoke, in a hushed, evil whisper. "Here's what we're going to do, Ms. Wright. Listen to me carefully. First, wipe these trifling, idealized messages off the Internet and block their computer from transmitting any more. Send a reverse virus to infect their little laptop – wipe their hard drive out."

Nathan was seething. His secret must be kept.

"Second, place a call to those motorcycle ruffians in St. Paul, the ones we used before to clean up mistakes and take care of witnesses..."

"You mean the Steel Serpents," Miranda said. She never forgot anything.

"Yes, exactly," he continued. "Locate the cabin this interloping family is staying in and send the biker gang up there to make sure they are never able to report what they saw again. Pay them double what we did last time."

"Yes, sir," Miranda replied. She was anxious to place the call. Her blood ran nearly as cold as his.

"And one more thing," he continued with a raspy hiss. "Bring in Colonel Shaka. Tell him to hunt down every last one of these black lynxes and wipe them off the planet. I never want to hear about this again."

"It will be my pleasure, Nathan," Miranda said, her voice elevated with excitement over the mission she was instrumental in initiating. "Everything will be taken care of by the time you get home. Everything."

By now, the four mammals and their feathered friend that make up the Natural Forces had meandered a few miles along the forgotten trail. The day was turning out to be magnificent weather-wise and they hadn't had to duck for cover from any humans for almost two hours now. The animals knew that if anyone saw the five of them hanging out together – especially with them all wearing special magical amulets - that it would draw too much attention and raise a lot of suspicion. They preferred to keep their secret as earth's guardians safe.

Cedar broke the quiet lull with a question. "So, Mesquite, we haven't seen a clue as to where we should be headed for quite some time now," the little badger said. "Just where exactly are you leading us?"

Mesquite turned to face the group while he continued plodding along the scenic trail. "I'm not sure, really," he said. "Guess we'll know it when we get there!"

"Wh-wh-what kind of answer is that?" Sequoia asked. "We can't just wander around the forest forever. I'm feeling a nap coming on..."

Aspen flew down and landed on Sequoia's back. He jumped a bit when he felt her little talons dig into his fur.

"A nap? You have got to be kidding!" she said. "You can

nap in the nighttime, Sequoia. I say we keep going this way for awhile and if we don't find anything, then I'll take over and you all can follow me."

Mesquite immediately jumped into the conversation to try to reassert himself as their non-elected leader. "No way, Aspen! We are not following you again. The last time we let you lead, you took us across a swamp and through some farmer's pasture. I'm still trying to grow back the fur I left on his barbed wire fence!"

"Hey, it's not my fault you guys can't fly over and around things," she said smartly. "You were all born grounders and I was born a flier. Naturally, that means in many ways I am better than you so it seems to me that I should be leading all…"

Cedar, the most short-tempered of the bunch, snapped at his falcon friend and interrupted her in mid-sentence. "Now hold it right there, featherhead! Just because you can fly doesn't mean you're better than us. I'd rather be down here with my four feet on the ground than with your two skinny feet on a tree branch and I'm sure the rest of us agree with me.

"I say we follow Mesquite for a little longer and then once he's finally admitted that he's lost, someone else can lead for awhile."

"Lost?" Mesquite said defensively. "What makes you think that I'm going to get us lost? And just who do you think should take over as trail leader? Juniper?"

"Hey!" Juniper snapped. "Don't drag me into this! I could be a leader as good as any of you, Mesquite! Just because I'm the youngest and the smallest doesn't mean a thing. I would make a good leader. Just watch me!"

"Would you all p-p-please just be quiet!" Sequoia bellowed. Now he was getting annoyed.

"Hey, man, she started it!" Cedar snapped back.

"I most certainly did not!" Aspen exclaimed.

Sequoia stopped and was staring off into the woods. He cocked his headed sideways and sniffed the air with his nose. Something was bothering him besides the group's bickering.

"If you all think you can do a better job than me," Mesquite proclaimed, " then just try. I am getting sick and tired of..."

"Shut up, already!" Sequoia yelled. "Listen!"

"Listen to what? I'm tired of listening to you guys!" Mesquite snapped. "You should all start listening to me for..."

"Shh!" Sequoia screamed at the others. "Just listen. Something's coming!"

*****

Less than 600 miles to the west, on a private ranch just outside of Pierre, South Dakota, Colonel Shaka's cell phone rang. It was Miranda Wright calling.

The fearless hunter was talking with the ranch owner on the porch of his lodge. Colonel Shaka came there every year to hunt down the biggest bison in the herd that roamed the rancher's 10,000-acre private reserve not far away.

Shaka excused himself, reached into his vest and flipped open the phone. "This is Colonel Shaka," he said, in his deep baritone voice and ever-present South African accent.

"Colonel, we have a mission for you," Miranda offered. "Sorry to interrupt your hunt, but this is coming from Mr. Axxes himself."

Shaka was disturbed. He enjoyed hunting buffalo and even killed a large one two years ago using just his Bowie knife, but he knew better than to disobey Nathan Axxes. And he paid him very well.

"What is the quarry this time?" he asked.

"Shouldn't be too tough for you – it's a lynx. A black lynx," she said.

"Miranda, there is no such thing. I have hunted every large cat in the world. There is no black lynx," the Colonel stated.

"Well, apparently a new species showed up and we need to make sure that these freaks of nature become extinct before they become discovered and protected," she explained.

"The thought of hunting down a whole new species and wiping them off the map sounds thrilling," Shaka mused.

"Where is this place?"

"Not too far from where you are now," she answered. "Upper Minnesota; I'll relay the coordinates to your cell."

"Very good, Ms. Wright," he replied.

"We are pulling three squads of Soldierjacks clearing a forest in south-central Minnesota. They are yours to command," Miranda said.

Her last comment agitated him. "You know I work alone," he growled. "I don't need your robots. I hunt alone."

"Colonel, this is not optional," she replied. Miranda did not like being challenged. "Use the Soldierjacks to guard the perimeter, use them to flush the varmints, I don't really care how you use them, but they're already en route. This is a high-priority hunt, Colonel. We need this taken care of fast and thoroughly. Nothing of their existence must remain. Nothing. We want these things completely eradicated."

"For the honor of being the sole person to erase a species, I will do as you say, Ms. Wright," the great hunter said. "I will leave immediately."

"And one more thing, Colonel Shaka," Miranda said with extra clarity in her voice. "No evidence of the black lynx must remain. That means no pelts, no taxidermy and no heads on your trophy wall. I'm talking about genocide, Colonel. Extinction."

The towering African man smiled, revealing a goldtooth that glinted in the sun. "I understand. Consider it done."

Sequoia's senses were correct. Something was coming. The earth below them was trembling ever so slightly and a raucous roar of multiple engines, their exhausts wide open, echoed like thunder through the forest. Flocks of birds took to wing as the train of motorcycles approached. Squirrels skittered up high into the trees or fled into their holes.

The Natural Forces team scampered through some brush on a small knoll in front of them that offered a better look at the approaching bikers. They were still at least a mile away. The roar from the bikes had completely shattered the calm and quiet of the peaceful forest. It was an interruption most unwelcome.

Below them, through a thick patch of birch trees, they could see a rustic, charming little log cabin. It sat in a sort of clearing, with clumps of wild grasses and wildflowers surrounding it. A newer deck wrapped around two sides of it with a small picnic table on it. It was a pristine setting, almost like a painting.

A thin, wispy trail of white smoke scrolled out of the river-rock chimney and dissipated into the air above it. The occupants were obviously burning some wood in the fireplace.

A modern blue mini-van was parked alongside it and, just a few yards away, a young boy was swinging on an old tire that hung from a large pine tree by a thick, braided fiber rope.

The five animals could see that a gravel road snaked away from the cabin and out through the forest in the direction of the approaching motorcycle gang. It was the only way in and the only way out. This cabin was truly remote.

At the sound of the approaching motorcycles, the boy stretched his feet to the ground and used his sneakers to stop the motion of his swinging, kicking up a small cloud of dust as he did so. He was puzzled by the oncoming ominous sound but also a little frightened. He hopped out of the tire swing and headed back into the relative safety of the cabin.

Inside, the kid found his father and mother gathered around their laptop computer at the small kitchen table. They were frustrated and agitated. Their personal computer had somehow lost its cellular Internet service and the operating system was refusing to boot up.

Before their son could even say anything, they heard the rumble of the motorcycles looming down on them and went to the window to see for themselves.

"I'm scared," the boy said and moved next to his father at the window. His mother put her arm around him. "Me too," she said, "me too."

In less than a minute, the procession of motorcycles invaded the serenity of the peaceful cabin in the woods. From his concealed place in the woods, Mesquite counted thirteen bikers in total.

They instantly started whooping and hollering as they formed a moving circle around the cabin, their tires tearing up the land around it. They gunned their throttles with reckless abandon and were clearly having a great time harassing the huddled family inside.

Then their leader – a huge, hulking man who eerily resembled an evil Santa Claus dressed in leather and denim and dark sunglasses – raised his fist in the air and signaled the entire motorcycle gang to stop. In nearly perfect unison, the swirling, disorderly horde grabbed for their brakes and came to a grinding halt. A cloud of dust encircled the cabin and rose slowly up in the air. Every motorcycle was aimed at the cabin, their headlights shining on it like beacons of impending disaster.

Their leader shut off his bike and used his huge left boot to snap out his kickstand. He cranked his handlebars to the left, leaned his chopper over and stepped off his two-wheeler. He turned and pointed at two others from his gang with his gloved hand.

They jumped off their bikes as well and walked over to the family's van. Each one of them reached into a pocket in their jeans and pulled out a switchblade knife. With a flick of their thumbs, a silvery blade snapped out into

the light. Amongst cheers from the rest of the group, they rammed their blades into the van's tires, slashing huge rips in them. Bursts of air hissed out against their legs as the van crouched low and lopsided into the dirt.

Other bikers stepped off their rides and pulled out tire irons, chains and even a baseball bat that had obviously been used multiple times recently to bash more than baseballs.

One particularly skinny biker, wearing what looked like an old Nazi helmet with a tall spike on top, reached into his motorcycle's saddlebag and produced two clear glass bottles with rags dangling out of their spouts. He called over to a thickly bearded buddy who had just lit a cigarette that dangled loosely from his lips.

Inside the cabin, the family sought protection by locking themselves in the innermost room, a small windowless bathroom. Even over the rumble of the idling motorcycles, sounds of the woman screaming and the child crying could be heard. The father, clutching his family to his chest, was desperately trying to call for help on his cell phone, but he was strangely not getting a signal.

"This stops now!" Mesquite turned and shouted to the others who were watching the mayhem from the knoll.

"'Bout time," Cedar shot back with a smile.

From within the forest, the Natural Forces team transformed into their super-selves. Bursts of turquoise light erupted all around, casting bizarre shadows of the

trees all around. Crazy reflections sparkled off the leaves. The bikers were too busy focused on their target to even notice.

The scrawny biker with the spiked helmet raised his bottle filled with gasoline over his head. His friend had just used a cigarette to set the rag dangling from it on fire. He was now holding a firebomb and he was going to throw it through a window in the cabin.

Suddenly, bright bluish-green projectiles streaked in from above, one of them shattering the fuel-filled bottle in his hand. Shards of glass exploded around the biker and the firebomb exploded just outside of his hand, knocking him to the ground.

Aspen, soaring in from above, had launched a volley of mystically powered feather-missiles, striking with typically brutal accuracy. The battle was on.

Juniper, lightning quick, propelled herself out of the brush and dashed into the biker gang in a turquoise colored blur. She zipped under, over and into a trio of bikers, smacking them hard and fast, knocking them into their bikes and into each other.

Mesquite and Sequoia burst out of the woods and joined the fray. Brandishing his magical staff, the superpowered wolf-warrior leaped between two bikers. In one quick move, he swept one of the leather-clad thugs off his feet and hard to the ground while smashing the other guy across the chest and sending him flying.

Sequoia, now a massive, humanistic grizzly, used his powerful arms to slam and fling whatever bikers were in his way to the side. Bodies of the seemingly tough motorcyclists flew all around him like rag dolls.

Realizing they were under attack by some crazed animals, the leader of the bikers reached into his jacket and pulled out a revolver. He cocked back the hammer and swung it up at Mesquite who had just dropkicked a biker across the picnic table and off the deck.

Just as he was about to pull the trigger, the ground in front of him erupted and a man-sized badger with claws the size of steak knives burst out of the hole. With one swift swipe, Cedar cut the handgun to shreds in the evil Santa's hand. Then with his left hand, he threw a powerful punch into the biker's gut, which knocked him to his knees, gasping for breath.

"Pick on someone your own size," Cedar growled at him and then knocked him out cold with a fist across his white-bearded jowls. The biker landed hard in the dust, face first. Cedar looked down at the big man and noticed his leather jacket was emblazoned with the words "Steel Serpents." He chuckled.

On the other side of the cabin, the two goons who had used their knives to slash the van's tires were standing back to back, holding their daggers protectively in front of them.

"Get back, you freaky animals! Back off or we'll cut

you!" one of them screamed. He was terrified.

Aspen swooped down from her aerial position at full speed. Just as she came down over the two men, she pulled up, lowered her legs and grabbed the man by his shoulders with her huge talons. Then, with a few hearty flaps of her 14-foot wingspan, she swooped back up into the sky, carrying the petrified man below her who was now screaming like a baby. Up and up they flew, over the roof of the cabin, and then she dropped him into a large pine tree. He fell hard, smacking against every limb on his way to the ground where he finally landed in an unconscious, battered pile of torn blue jeans and shredded leather jacket parts.

The remaining knife wielder threw his knife to the ground and ran to his chopper. He jumped on board, fired it up and took off in a hurry. Juniper laughed and shot after him. Before he got very far, the speedy super-powered ferret ran right up next to him, jumped up onto the gas tank, reached down, pulled out the keys and jumped back off.

The motorcycle violently shuddered to a stop and the completely startled biker lost all control. He crashed it hard into a ditch, hurling himself headlong over the handlebars and into a thorny patch of raspberry bushes.

Two more bikers leaped onto their metal steeds and followed suit. They gunned their engines and bolted from the scene only to be met in the road by Mesquite who

leaped in front of them, held up his staff and clothes-lined them both off their bikes and flat onto their backs in a whirlwind of dust and pain.

Sequoia stepped around the corner of the cabin to find a heavy-set biker wearing a cut-off jean-jacket swirling a long, heavy chain over his head. He looked angry.

The mighty grizzly brought up his magical shield just as the chain came smashing down, aimed directly at his face. It smacked hard against his shield and bounced off harmlessly.

"Oh, you shouldn't have done that, little man!" the bear bellowed as he turned and picked up a chopper by its front forks. Then, like a tennis racket, he swatted the biker with the heavy machine and sent him tumbling across the property, broken and battered.

Only one of the Steel Serpents remained – a woman with a red bandana tied around her head. She was standing a few yards in front of the tire swing with a lead pipe clutched in her hand. She was heavily tattooed and wearing motorcycle boots with extra tall heels and a pair of tattered jeans that were entirely too tight.

"I d-d-don't know what you creatures are," the biker chick said with a fear-induced stutter that made Sequoia snicker when he heard it. "B-b-but if you come near me, I'll knock your heads off!"

Aspen, Juniper, Mesquite and Sequoia slowly walked

toward her, and she slowly stepped backward as she watched them move in.

Then, unexpectedly, Cedar popped up behind her. He grabbed the tire swing and slammed it down over her head and shoulders until it came to rest, jammed at her midsection with her arms stuck inside. He then whipped the swing with its hapless occupant dangling within and it spun out of control, banging occasionally against the tree as it pivoted around on its rope axis. It was too much for the brawny biker woman who passed out from the rough ride after shrieking for nearly two minutes.

Before morphing back into their younger forms, the Natural Forces team tossed most of the bikers out onto the gravel road, a safe distance away from the cabin. Sequoia had stacked the gang's motorcycles into a pile of twisted metal and broken glass that was nearly as tall as a tree.

The Steel Serpents that were able to walk limped away from the scene, carrying or dragging their unconscious gang members with them. They were in shock at what had happened. Nobody would believe them.

Once the whole lot was far enough away, the five animals came back to check on the cabin to make sure those inside were unhurt. After realizing the family of victims was indeed fine, and they were confident that the bikers wouldn't be coming back, the group retreated back into the forest.

They were glad they had been there at the right place at the right time. But they also knew something wasn't right. They could sense a storm was brewing, but not the kind that comes from the sky.

Colonel Shaka stepped out of the Axxes corporate helicopter into the fresh air of the Superior National Forest. As he walked away from the whirling blades, he had to stoop over since his impressive frame put his head awfully close to the spinning rotors.

He carried two very large, fully loaded duffel bags under each arm as he strutted over to a series of tents surrounded by several Axxes-supplied Soldierjacks. This was base camp. The helicopter lifted off when the pilot could see its very important passenger was clear.

Shaka is a colossal man. Tall and immensely muscular, he resembled a defensive end in professional football. Nathan Axxes recruited him several years ago in Shaka's homeland of South Africa when he was just 20 years old. Back then, Axxes needed some enforcers around his diamond mines and Shaka was leading a group of soldiers-for-hire.

Warlords are common in several politically disrupted sections of the African continent and Shaka bullied, manipulated and fought his way to the top. As warlord, he gave himself the rank of colonel and ruled over many sectors with a brutal, merciless style. By the time Nathan Axxes came calling, Shaka was leading a small

army of mercenaries and building himself an empire of power and riches through corruption and fear.

Shaka's soldiers worked for the Axxes Conglomeration for many years. They served as overseers of the miners and kept them from forming labor unions or striking. They guarded the mines, punished thieves and trespassers and even strong-armed their way into more territory to start up more mines.

Eventually, Colonel Shaka grew tired of serving as the leader of the Axxes security force in South Africa. He soon roamed outside his duties and responsibilities, hunting down those who Axxes wanted silenced. He found great excitement in these excursions and asked for more and more assignments of the lethal sporting type.

After eliminating, or intimidating, all those who stood in the evil corporation's way, Shaka turned his sights on big game hunting. He soon became an expert tracker and with the advanced technology exclusively at his disposal through his new employer, Colonel Shaka found himself armed with high-tech weaponry, traps and devices.

Shaka's bloodlust was unquenchable. He had hunted every sizable animal species on the continent: lion, cape buffalo, zebra, hyena, oryx and hippopotamus. Soon, even protected species appeared in his crosshairs: cheetahs, leopards, rhinos, elephants and gorillas.

After a while, he realized that his weaponry was too good. His kills were too easy. He needed to be challenged.

He craved the thrill of the hunt, but only when real danger was involved. He wanted to be closer to his kills, take their lives while up close and personal.

Colonel Shaka started taking experimental injections to keep up with his prey and become more involved in the chase. He devoured supplements and poured elixirs down his throat if he thought they would help increase his stamina, strength and agility. He was becoming superhuman. They were also driving him mad.

Not long ago, Shaka read about a massive crocodile that had been spotted in Tanzania. A true monster, it was reported that this Nile crocodile was a 20-foot-long, two thousand-pound leviathan. He decided to hunt it down.

After weeks of tracking the beast with little success, Shaka made a bold decision. On the outskirts of a nearby village, the frustrated huntsman kidnapped a 10-year-old boy and used him as bait. Tying the child to a tiny, flimsy raft, Shaka watched in delight as the crocodile finally made its appearance after two days of waiting; no doubt lured by the cries and thrashings of the youngster.

He caught the giant reptile in a trap and pounced on it armed only with a spear. Intent on stabbing it through the heart, Shaka moved in for the kill. But the crocodile broke free and during its struggle to escape from the savage hunter, its gnashing teeth and smashing tail nearly killed the Colonel.

Shaka managed to crawl away where he lay bleeding for hours in the filthy mud along the shoreline. Nearly dead, he was finally rescued by Axxes operatives who were monitoring his every move. Weeks in the hospital kept Shaka alive, but his right eye was lost permanently.

Nathan Axxes made the Colonel an offer he could not refuse. In exchange for permanent status as an exclusive corporate henchman, the company would rebuild him. Axxes wanted an assassin he could trust on his staff, someone to do the company's dirty work whenever they needed.

Medical scientists and technological wizards reconstructed the African warlord-turned-hunter. Hidden underneath a red titanium eye path, a sophisticated ocular scope was bolted into his eye socket that provided long-distance sight as well as thermal imaging and night vision capabilities.

His torn, infected muscles were mended and enhanced with alloy mesh materials integrated into his body and his broken bones were bonded with a metallic coating. In a few months, Colonel Shaka was more powerful than he could have ever imagined.

Under his agreement, the Colonel dedicated himself to the Axxes Conglomeration and moved to its corporate headquarters in California. There, he carried out secretive and deadly jobs with a skill and effectiveness never before seen.

During periods between assignments, he trained with martial artists, Special Forces soldiers and experts in field operations. He also designed his own weaponry and traps, using the futuristic capabilities and unlimited funds in the Axxes research and development labs. He became the feared and respected right-hand-man to Nathan Axxes himself.

As he stepped into the larger of the base camp tents, he dropped his heavy duffel bags to the ground. Glancing around, Colonel Shaka could see the Soldierjacks had already set up his sleeping quarters, a field desk and collapsible chair as well as a row of folding tables that supported several large flat-screen monitors hooked into a variety of computers. Three large containers were lined up on the other side of the tent.

"Good. I see you brought the gear I asked for," the Colonel said with his South African dialect flavoring every word. He always got upset when others confused his accent as being British or Australian. "This should be a simple hunt, mates. Bait, traps, snares. Easy stuff!"

He had worked with all versions of the Soldierjack worker drones. Despite their limited speech capabilities, standard issue Soldierjacks only spoke when asked direct questions or while on sentry duty. Shaka felt obliged to speak. They seemed human enough and he liked pleasant conversation when in the company of others because when he was hunting he often went for days

without uttering a word or making a noise.

He walked over to a topographical map that was pinned with tacks to a large, vertically standing corkboard. Next to it was the latest satellite imagery of the area they were in. The corporation had access to military satellites, without the government's permission, of course.

Colonel Shaka assessed the land and began formulating placement of his traps. He slowly stroked the triangular-shaped goatee on his chin as he brooded over his plan. At the same time, he plotted where he would position the platoon of Soldierjacks to keep any wandering humans away—with force if necessary.

In less than an hour, he had his strategy fully designed. The map now contained different colored pushpins that indicated exactly what went where. Blue pins were traps, green ones were motion-activated sensors tied into cameras and red ones indicated where the Soldierjacks would be positioned. In all, twelve square miles were covered for his initial hunt.

He then opened one of his duffel bags and dumped the contents out on the bed. Sifting through them, he laid out his clothing and gear for the pending hunt. Next, he opened the three large steel containers the Soldierjacks had brought with them earlier. Inside, a large assortment of weapons and equipment were at his disposal. He selected a few items and set them down next to his cot.

In a few moments, he had changed into his hunting

garb and headed back to the map. He looked truly impressive, as if he was ready for war.

"All right, 'jacks, gather around," the Colonel ordered in a booming voice. "Select your positions and synchronize based on the coordinates on the map. Ten of you will stay back here and run the base camp – feed me any info you get through my headset. I want the large titanium cage set up in tent number three; I am expecting to catch these things alive. I know some people overseas that pay me handsomely for exotic animals and know how to keep a secret.

"Once the perimeter is set, nobody gets in or out. No witnesses. If you see the cats I'm after, call it in. Do not engage. These lynxes are mine to deal with, not yours.

"I estimate our mission to take less than 48 hours. This should be a walk in the park, troops. I don't anticipate any problems."

With that, the Soldierjacks coordinated amongst themselves through wireless computerized transmission and moved out to take up their positions.

Colonel Shaka picked up his equipment and set out to install his traps. A wide grin stretched across his dark brown, usually scowling face. He loved to hunt.

A few hours later, the Natural Forces younglings found themselves awakening from a nap. Pleading from Sequoia had finally convinced the others that some rest under a fat fir tree was just what they all needed and too tempting to resist. They had hunkered down on the soft bed of old, decaying pine needles and dozed off to sleep.

It was Juniper's yelps that awoke the others.

"Juniper, what's wrong?" Mesquite asked with sleepy eyes.

"Ants!" Juniper screamed. "They're everywhere! Biting me!" She was up and dancing about, shaking herself to get them off.

The others started laughing at her plight.

"You should have thick fur like us, little girl," Cedar said as he fought back a chuckle. "Ants don't bother me much!"

"Yeah, yeah," Juniper snapped back. "Can you imagine what a black-footed ferret would look like with thick fur? I'd look like a two-foot-long chinchilla wearing a mask."

That comment made the gang laugh even more.

Aspen, who had been napping on a branch above the others, peered down and spoke up, "How about we head over to the river, everyone? We can drink some water and Juniper can wash the rest of the ants out of her fur!" She was being semi-serious but couldn't help but giggle

as she said it.

"Well, I c-c-could sure go for a drink," Sequoia said as he stretched his pudgy frame and released a big yawn.

"Me too," Mesquite said. "C'mon, Juniper, let's get out of here. You okay now?"

She shivered one last time. "Sure. Stupid ants!"

The five of them crawled out from under the shade of the evergreen and plodded through the wild grass down toward the river. It was late afternoon.

The Vermilion River is a large waterway that flows out of Crane Lake in a jaggedly western direction. A canoer's paradise, the river offers some spectacular scenery and a wide variety of thin and wide spots.

At one of the narrower stretches, the fivesome pushed aside some thickets at the water's edge to lap up the cool water from a side pool formed by an old log and some larger rocks. It was clean, fresh water and they felt energized after filling themselves on it.

Mesquite noticed something on the ground nearby.

"Hey, guys, look at this!" he exclaimed.

The gang gathered around.

"Check out these tracks in the mud. They look…feline," Mesquite said.

"And big!" Sequoia said as he put his considerably large paw in the footprint. "This is an aw-aw-awfully large cat!"

"Lemme see that," Cedar said with a hint of disbelief in

his voice. He barged his way into the gaggle for a closer look. "Wow. You're not kiddin'. Those are some fat feet."

"Do you think it's a mountain lion?" Juniper asked, with more than a little fear in her tone.

"Cougars around here are very rare," Aspen said assuredly. She liked to show off her intelligence. "It's probably a bobcat. A really big bobcat."

Mesquite's ears popped up and an excited look sprung across his face. "Hey, let's follow the tracks! Let's go find him and mess with him! Maybe we can sneak up on him and scare him!"

"What?" Juniper practically screamed. "I don't want to go chasing some big cat around the forest. And I'm sure Aspen doesn't want to either."

Aspen flittered up one branch higher than she was before. In her morphed state, she could easily take on a large wildcat but as a small bird, she could end up as its food just as quickly. She didn't want the others to think she was scared so she went along with Mesquite's offer, despite her better judgement.

"Yeah, sure, I'll go," she said.

"Count me in!" Cedar added. He was getting bored anyway.

"Me too," Sequoia said. "I g-g-gotta see just how big this c-c-cat is!"

Juniper, propped up on her back haunches, crossed her arms in disgust. "This is really stupid, you guys."

With that, Mesquite bounded off, following the footprints as they veered away from the shoreline and up into the woods.

In short order, the paw prints from the feline had completely disappeared as the natural forest flooring hardened and made it less favorable to leave impressions in the ground. Mesquite and the others instead looked for pathways the cat had pushed through the grass, the occasional tuft of black hair they found snagged on a twig or even Sequoia's rather powerful sense of smell.

After a couple of miles or so of meandering around in the woods, they came across a shadowy gulley. Large, rotting logs and moss-covered stumps were scattered about. This was old, untouched forest. It was deep in the timber, quiet and dark.

The five creatures in pursuit of the wildcat all paused as they looked upon it. This seemed like perfect bobcat habitat.

"Something's not right here, guys," Cedar said. He bared his teeth a little as he scanned the area.

"Say what?" Mesquite said in disbelief. "Now you are scared too? I can see the bird and the ferret getting frightened by a stupid cat, but a badger? C'mon, Cedar, quit being a chicken. Cats like to eat chicken!"

After proudly razzing his badger pal, the wolf pup wandered straight down into the shadowy ravine, no doubt as an act of bravery for his friends to see.

Primeval ferns grew in the cool shade and fragrant earth, as did a large colony of mushrooms. Mesquite pushed past the plant life and plodded on down to the bottom of the gulley.

Suddenly, something whipped through the leaves and launched straight up into the air with a horrible scream.

It was Mesquite! His paw had triggered a rope snare that snatched his leg and whipped him up high above the gulley, swinging upside down from the cord tied to the trees above.

After realizing he was fine, but most certainly embarrassed, his four friends busted out in laughter. Cedar lost all control and rolled over onto his back, laughter roaring from deep inside so hard that his eyes started watering.

Mesquite just swung there back and forth like a pendulum, six feet off the forest floor, his arms folded against his chest in disgust and bewilderment. He was mightily embarrassed.

After some more teasing, and thorough enjoyment of the situation, Aspen flew up and landed on Mesquite's captured leg. It took her awhile, but using her beak and talons, she managed to cut her wolf friend loose.

Mesquite fell to the ground with a thump, which of course caused more giggling amongst his pals.

"Alright, alright already," Mesquite bemoaned. "Hardy-har-har. While you all were so busy laughing, I was up

there thinking about just what a snare is doing out here in the middle of the woods anyway?"

There was a moment of silence as the fivesome thought about it.

From out of nowhere came a whisper. "I think they're trying to catch us," said a tiny voice from a hollow log near where Mesquite had just landed.

A pair of small, darkly colored identical lynx kittens stepped out for all to see. They had rather large paws for such small bodies and their ears sprouted extra long tufts of hair that pointed straight up. They were shy and scared.

Gasping, the Natural Forces companions stepped back in shock. They weren't expecting this.

Juniper then leaned forward. "Who are you guys? Where is your mother?"

The black cub that spoke earlier stepped even closer. "My sister and I are black lynxes," the little male said proudly. He was slightly cross-eyed. "We are really rare. Our mom told us that we're the only ones south of the Canadian border and nobody even knows we exist. At least until now, that is."

"I guess so," Juniper replied in a friendly tone. She could see they were too young to be on their own. Since she was small like them, she thought she could establish a trust. "Where is your mother?"

"The mean man came and took her," the little female

said. "He caught her in a trap just like the one your friend found. We were with her when it happened. We couldn't get her down. And then the big man with the red eye came. He tied her feet and put her in a cage. She told us to run..." The lynx kitten broke off her sentence and started sobbing.

"Hush now, it'll be alright," her brother said, trying to sooth her. "These animals are here to help." He looked at the five strangers with sad, desperate eyes. "You are going to help us, aren't you?"

Mesquite walked forward, and the others followed. "Of course, we're going to help you guys," he said. "Now where is the last place you saw your mother?"

Nervously, the lynx kittens took the others to where their mother had been captured. It was about a mile away. When they got there, they could see the rope that had snared her just a few hours earlier now hung empty. It dangled from a tall birch tree, slowly swaying back and forth in the breeze.

The infant cats started sobbing when they saw the scene. It was too much for them to handle.

The group backed away slowly from the area and gathered together under a red pine tree. It seemed safe for now.

By unanimous decision, the Natural Forces animals decided they should split up. They couldn't take any chances. The man who was hunting them seemed very skilled and it should be assumed that he knew about the

twins and would probably come after them next.

The first team, made up of Mesquite, Sequoia and Aspen, would go after the mother lynx and try to free her from the hunter-trapper with the red eye. The second team, just Juniper and Cedar, would escort the lynx kittens away from the area and head north back across the border. It wasn't going to be easy.

"We'll find your mother," Mesquite said to the black lynx cubs, presuming it wasn't going to be an empty promise. "Don't worry. We'll get her back and meet you in the northern nation."

Then Mesquite turned to Cedar and Juniper. "When you get there, go to the tallest tree on the highest hill. We'll find you."

"Got it," Juniper acknowledged.

Mesquite had one more thing to say. "It's going to be dark soon, so I suggest when night falls, that you bunk down somewhere and restart in the morning. Now go. And be careful. There's probably traps everywhere."

Cedar snickered. "Hah! You're the one who better be careful, pup! You seem to have a hankerin' for finding snares more than the rest of us!"

"We'll be alright," Aspen interjected, defending her friend, but also making sure the kittens wouldn't think that they would fail on their mission of freeing their mother. "Just take care of those little ones."

Juniper, Cedar and the lynx kittens turned and walked

slowly and carefully toward the north. Juniper looked back at her three other friends as she crested a small mound sprouting evergreen saplings. "Goodbye, you guys. We'll see you soon!" she said humbly and hopefully.

With that, the four of them disappeared into the thick forest.

"We got t-t-to find their mother," Sequoia said to Mesquite and Aspen. "We just gotta."

"Yeah, I know," Mesquite replied. He was worried. Then he turned in the other direction and moved out cautiously along with the bear cub and young falcon, following the trapper's huge boot prints in the forest floor.

On the horizon, just behind the tree line, the sun was sinking low and the temperature was dipping. The forest's orchestra of frogs, crickets and night birds was just getting started.

The forest at sundown is a difficult place to navigate. The heavy canopy of trees blocks out most of what little light is available from the rising moon and setting sun, while the towering tree trunks create long, ebony shadows and effectively paint the entire place with giant black strokes.

Negotiating this dark wilderness, Cedar and Juniper, along with their two feline wards, found progress to be incredibly slow. They had already come across two more traps that were set by this mysterious hunter and managed to not just avoid them, but also spring them harmlessly so no others would fall victim to his trickery.

In the exact opposite direction, Mesquite, Sequoia and Aspen weren't faring much better. The hunter's trail had gone cold rather quickly. His boot steps were nearly impossible to find on the shadowy forest floor and he left almost no telltale sign of his presence. His scent was undetectable and he seemed to move with extra care so as not to break any of the leaves and branches in his wake. He was a stealthy human.

Fortunately, his quarry – the mother lynx – was easier to detect. Her scent was distinguishable, barely, through the thick wood. It took extreme concentration

for Mesquite and Sequoia to detect the microscopic particles she left in the air.

Flying above them, Aspen did her best, peering into the darkness from a higher elevation to try to find the man with the captured cat. Her vision was the keenest of them all, but she was severely hampered in the night. It was like trying to find a green crayon in a field of grass.

All of a sudden, Sequoia smelled something. "Hold up!" the bear cub exclaimed. "C-c-can you smell that?" he asked Mesquite.

The wolf pup strained his neck and moved his nose through the cool, night air. "Yeah," he replied. "It smells like trout!"

"C'mon!" Sequoia blurted and bounded off in the direction of the smell. He was hungry and Mesquite was also. They had hardly eaten all day.

Aspen swooped down. She hollered down to her furry friends, romping through the woods with great abandon. Something wasn't right. "Trout? Out here in the middle of nowhere? Guys! Listen to me! This is a trap!"

Ignoring her, the boys came to a small opening in the trees. On a stump in front of them, aglow in the moonlight, lay a two-foot-long, meaty lake trout. It must have been caught earlier that day. It was still fresh.

"Look at that!" Mesquite exclaimed.

"Halfsies!" Sequoia declared. The two of them moved in for their late-night snack.

Aspen flew down and circled around the stump while calling out to her friends who were clearly blinded by hunger. "Stop! Stay where you are! Don't you think this is a trap? Why would there be a big ol' trout out here in the middle of the forest? Think about it!"

The bear and the wolf stopped dead in their tracks. They looked each other in the eyes. They didn't want to believe her.

Mesquite thought of a rational explanation. "Well," he said, "what if an eagle had caught this trout earlier today and was bringing it back to its nest and then accidentally dropped it? That could be it. A stupid eagle dropped it!"

Aspen couldn't believe what she was hearing. "Seriously? That is the explanation you're willing to risk your life for? Seriously?"

Sequoia's stomach was grumbling. "I c-c-could see that. Eagles d-d-drop things all the time."

Aspen was getting frustrated. These boys could not see past their stomachs. She flew over to them and landed on a protruding branch nearby. "Really? Really? Have you ever even seen an eagle? C'mon, Sequoia, don't tell me you're that stupid."

"Well, this hunter-man didn't use bait for his other trap," Mesquite interjected. "I have a hard time believing it's the same guy. Besides, there's no trees close enough to it to tie his stupid rope for his stupid snare."

"C'mon, Aspen," Sequoia pleaded. 'We're st-st-starving here."

"I swear, you guys don't have a single brain between the two of you," Aspen said spitefully. Then she paused and decided to make a deal. She was hungry, too. "Okay. How about this... I weigh the least of all of us. So, I will fly over there and see if I can find the trap. If not, I will try to push that trout off the stump because it's obviously too big for me to lift."

"Okay!" Mesquite hurriedly agreed.

"Yeah, good p-p-plan!" Sequoia said, licking his lips in anticipation.

"If anything happens to me, you two idiots better rescue me," Aspen replied. "Right away. No dilly-dallying either. Promise?"

"Yeah, yeah, we promise," Mesquite said for both of them. "Now go. I'm dying here!"

Aspen launched herself off the twig she was perched on and soared around the stump for a few times. It seemed all clear.

With a deep breath, she hovered in and landed ever so gently on the stump right next to the plump trout.

As soon as she landed, a perfect circle of 40 steel bars shot straight up from the ground. They formed a cage around the stump, ten-feet high and crackling with some sort of electrical charge. There was less then three inches of space between each one.

"You see?" Aspen shouted from inside the cage. "I told you this was a trap! I told you so! Now get me out of here!"

After recovering from being startled by the trap, Mesquite and Sequoia started chuckling. Aspen's plight was a small one indeed.

"Look up, Aspen," Mesquite said as he held back his laughter. "Who's an idiot now? There's no roof, just fly out of there."

Embarrassed and frustrated, the little peregrine falcon flew up and out of the encircled jail cell. She was angry but relieved at the same time. This could have gone much worse. She landed back on the branch next to her friends who were now dejected that their easy meal would not come to be.

"That trap was clearly set for an animal – not a bird," Aspen said, finally catching her breath.

"I agree," Mesquite said. "Just what kind of human hunter has access to these sort of traps? Who even makes stuff like this? This is no ordinary man we're up against here. This guy is dangerous. Very dangerous."

*****

Meanwhile, across the forest, the young badger, ferret and two lynx kittens had come across an old, abandoned iron-ore mine. It had been shut down for many years, and was sealed extremely well at the front entrance with some sort of fancy steel door. Strangely,

it was completely surrounded with multiple sets of razor wire. Somebody wanted this place left alone.

Cedar and Juniper agreed it would be an excellent place to hide out overnight. The baby lynxes were getting very tired and cranky. This would be a good place to catch up on some sleep and start again on their journey north in the morning when they had better visibility. And it seemed highly unlikely that the red-eyed trapper man would set any surprises in this place.

Juniper stayed with the kits as Cedar slowly checked around the site, trying to find a place to burrow in. After a short time, he came across an area where years of changing weather had taken their toll and created a small crevice between some large rocks. He wiggled his way in between the natural gap in the earth and started digging. Being a badger, even a young one, allowed him to tunnel at a rather quick pace and in short order, he had broken through into the mine itself.

He called the others over and showed them their new, temporary home. They clamored their way inside the cold, dark cavern and found a good place to rest. Gathering in a clump, the four animals curled up together and lay down to sleep. The baby lynxes immediately dozed off and one of them started snoring almost right away.

Off in the distance, a pair of owls was trying their best to contact each other, their hoots echoing disturbingly into the night. It was going to be a long, long evening, Cedar thought.

Morning came to the Northwoods in the warming embrace of the early sun. Birds were the first to rise and made sure all the animals in the forest were aware of their presence as their calls and chirps came at first light by the thousands.

Mesquite and Sequoia, slowly coming out of their slumber, looked up to the sky with a less than pleasant attitude. Aspen had already been awake for almost an hour. Last night, the three of them had pushed on another two miles past the trap they had sprung at the stump before finding shelter under a fallen tree where they had slept for the night. They hoped to find the mother lynx at dawn.

After an extremely deep yawn that involved his tongue flopping out and curling back in, Mesquite glanced up to Aspen in the evergreen above. "Why can't birds ever shut up?" he asked with a smirk.

"Humph! The early bird gets the worm, stupid grounder," she shot back. Then she turned her beak toward the sky, shunning the wolf pup even more.

"So, did you have worms for breakfast without us?" Mesquite cracked.

"Let's get go-go-going, guys," Sequoia stuttered. He

stood and stretched and then continued, "We promised those little ones that w-w-we'd find their mom."

*****

Simultaneously, six miles away, Cedar and Juniper were awakened by one of the little lynxes that was quite riled up.

"Wake up! Wake up!" the little cat cried out while prodding at the sleepy badger and ferret with her paws.

"What's wrong?" Juniper asked as she jumped to her feet. 'What's going on?"

"My sister went deeper into the mine shaft!" the little boy frantically reported. "I tried to stop her, but she wouldn't listen. She said she could hear water dripping and she wanted a drink. I told her to wait for you guys but she said she didn't have to. We have to go get her!"

"Geez, alright already," Cedar grumbled. He was especially grumpy in the morning. "Go get her, Juniper. I just need five more minutes of sleep." With that, he tucked himself up into a little black and white ball of bristly fur and fell back asleep.

Juniper rolled her eyes at her crabby cohort and headed back deeper into the mine with the scared little lynx close behind. "She's fine. We'll find her," Juniper said. "I'm kinda thirsty myself."

They walked a few steps further into the old mine

shaft and away from the crack of light that was peering into the opening Cedar had dug the night before. Soon Juniper could hear the plopping sound of water droplets hitting a puddle and echoing off the walls. It was very dark.

"Hello? Little lynx?" Juniper called out. She was deeply hoping nothing had happened to the little girl and that she hadn't gotten into any trouble.

"Back here!" a little voice called out. It was the lost lynx cub. "I found some cold, clear, fresh water! You're gonna love it!"

Juniper was relieved and she quickened her steps to find the lost wildcat in the darkness. In seconds, they were together again, at the edge of a small pool of water in a rocky depression at the back edge of the mineshaft. Their pupils were wide open, helping them to see in the pitch black, but even so, all the three of them could make out were shapes and movement.

"Please don't wander off without telling us," Juniper scolded the independent feline. "We have to stick together."

"Yes, ma'am," she replied, bowing her head.

"Well, since we're here…" Juniper said. She and the other little lynx couldn't resist and lapped up a few mouthfuls of the refreshing liquid.

"Told you I wasn't a scaredy-cat," the wandering sister sneered to her twin.

Her snide remark triggered a fight as one little cat pounced on the other. Juniper squinted her eyes and

peered down the inky-black passageway to watch them tussle harmlessly around in the darkness. It was innocent fun, until they accidentally rolled into an unseen sensor and triggered a horrific alarm.

Suddenly, two hidden overhead bright lights came on, blinding all three animals and flooding the whole passageway in brilliant, harsh light. It was like two small suns suddenly erupted in front of their eyes.

"Intruder alert! Intruder alert!" blared out loudly from somewhere in front of them. Something heavy and mechanical came alive and moved toward them.

The lynx kids started screaming. Juniper, holding her arm up over eyes to blot out the overwhelming lights, called out to them. "Over here! Follow my voice! Come to me!"

The lynx cubs somehow found Juniper and she clutched each one under each of her small arms. She knew it would be a few minutes before they had their vision back. They were all disoriented.

From a few yards inside the mineshaft, a whirring, crunching, clanking noise moved rapidly toward them. It sounded almost like a small tank.

"Intruder alert! Destroy! Destroy!" echoed down the carved corridor. It emanated from an Axxes-designed sentry droid. The man-made machine was a robot with a humanistic upper torso attached to an armored cart driven by two treads. The sentry's left arm formed into some kind of futuristic machine gun below the elbow and

its right had been replaced by a flamethrower. This droid was designed to protect and kill.

Juniper could tell she was in trouble. She heard the robot's weapon system activate and she could detect it was leveling them at her and the twins.

At the last second, on a sheer well-timed guess, she hurled herself and the kittens out of the way. The sentry's machine-gun arm opened up and fired a barrage right where the three animals had just been standing. The hail of bullets tore into the rocky ground and ricocheted off in all directions.

"Reacquire target. Destroy! Destroy!" the unstopping sentry's robotic voice affirmed. It whirled about for another blast with both weapons at the ready.

A sudden rush blew past Juniper and the kittens clutched to her sides. With an angry roar, Cedar, transformed into his warrior-self, slammed headlong into the mechanized sentinel. His claws were fully extended and glowing like neon-blue knives.

The robot wasn't prepared for the badger's charge and Cedar tore a gaping gash through its entire left side, severing its machine gun arm in the process.

"Systems damage! Systems damage! Destroy new intruder! Destroy new intruder!" the tank-bot bellowed.

It swung up its right arm and let loose a fiery cloud of scorching flames. Cedar dodged the hot blast by leaping out of the way and came up behind the track-driven

machine man for a final blow.

With a powerful swipe of his mystical claws, Cedar cut the sentry droid in half. Its body crashed headfirst into the stony floor. Electrical sparks erupted from its mortal wounds. After a few seconds, the bottom half ceased moving as well and the small, motorized treads stopped rotating.

"You three okay?" Cedar asked the others.

"Man, what took you so long?" Juniper said, with a sigh of relief. Her eyesight was just returning.

"Sorry," Cedar replied with a grin. "Guess I'm not a morning person."

The lynx cubs were in total shock. They could not believe what they just witnessed. They just stared at Cedar with their mouths wide open.

Looking around, Cedar noticed that down the mineshaft from where the drone attacked stood a steel door similar to the one on the outside. A large sign was plastered across it in bright red letters. "Do not enter. Trespassers will be shot."

Cedar smiled and walked up to the doorway. "What are they protecting so hard in here?" he thought.

He raised his right hand high over his head and slashed down hard across the metal door, ripping it open as if it were made of cardboard. Then he pushed it open further so he could step inside.

Juniper and the lynx cubs came up behind Cedar and

joined him on the other side of the torn doorway.

A large cavern opened up in front of them. It seemed to be the last shaft of the original iron-ore mine that had shut down operations dozens of years ago. But it was still being used for storage of the most dangerous kind.

Stacked inside were two large nuclear missile nose cones still attached to their warheads. They were all of an older design, and bigger in size than today's versions. They had been carefully set there, on custom-made racks, many years ago. A layer of dust covered each one but the nuclear symbols and the U.S. Air Force markings were still clearly visible.

"Are those what I think they are?" Juniper asked, stepping backwards. Cedar, who was in shock himself, nodded. "Yeah, I think so," he confirmed. "Nukes."

"What are nukes?" one of the lynx cubs asked.

"Don't ask, kid. You don't want to know," Juniper said. "Let's get out of here."

"We're losing his trail," Mesquite said to the others with a hint of desperation in his voice. "I can't detect the scent anymore and the red-eyed man's tracks have all but disappeared. This guy's good!"

"I agree," Sequoia said. "My s-s-sense of s-s-smell is really good and even I can't pick them up anymore."

Aspen fluttered down and landed next to the wolf pup and the bear cub. "I could maybe fly up high and try to spot them from the air but the tree canopy is too thick. I could be right over them and never see them. We need to try something else," she mentioned – a plan already hatched in her head.

"Like what?" Mesquite quipped.

"Maybe we should just ask," Aspen proudly proposed.

"Ask? Are you insane?" Mesquite erupted. "What are we supposed to do? Shout out over the whole forest and ask him where he is? I doubt he could hear us anyway and even if he did, he can't speak our animal language!"

"We don't ask the hunter, you moron; we ask the other animals of the forest if they've seen the hunter and which way he went," Aspen retorted.

A long pause hovered thick in the air.

Mesquite was clearly embarrassed. With his head

hung low, he cracked an apologetic smile across his face and in a hushed voice replied, "Oh, yeah, that might just work. When you said…I thought you meant…it didn't make sense…oh, never mind. Let's start askin' around." The little wolf stormed off.

Aspen looked up at Sequoia who was struggling to keep from laughing. "I swear his momma dropped him on his head when he was born," she said.

With that, Sequoia and Aspen bounded off after Mesquite who was scanning the woods for an animal friend who could bear witness to the whereabouts of the mysterious red-eyed hunter. After a few hundred yards, he spotted movement in the trees. It was a squirrel.

"Hey, you! Squirrel!" Mesquite shouted upwards into the birch tree. "I wanna ask you something! Come down here!"

The squirrel turned to look at the wolfling barking away at him on the forest floor. Confused, it flicked its tail in sharp angry movements as a warning for others and then it darted up higher in the tree, hidden in the branches somewhere.

"Hey!" Mesquite screamed angrily. "I'm talking to you, squirrel!"

Aspen and Sequoia finally caught up with Mesquite and sat down alongside him.

"D-d-did the squirrel say he saw anything?" the bear asked.

Mesquite furrowed his eyebrows. "No. He's scared or

something. He probably thought I was gonna eat him!"

"Let's move on," Aspen said. "And let me do the talkin' this time. I shouldn't scare them half to death like you are."

"Good idea," Mesquite replied. "You give it a try. Most animals are imitated by us wolves."

"You m-m-mean intimidated," Sequoia said, correcting his pal.

"What?" Mesquite snapped.

"Y-y-you said imitated b-b-but you meant to say intimidated," Sequoia repeated.

"That's what I said. Intimitated," Mesquite replied, trying to recover, but only making it worse.

"Intimidated," Sequoia said again, only slower and with extra emphasis on the syllables.

"Whatever!" Mesquite was visibly upset. "Let's just go find some stupid animals!"

"I think we found one already," Aspen quipped but in a hushed voice so Mesquite couldn't quite hear her. She figured he'd had enough already.

"Let's spread out a little. We can cover more ground that way and increase our chances of finding a fellow forest dweller who may have seen which way the huntsman went," Aspen proffered.

"Good idea," Sequoia said and meandered off to his left a few dozen yards. Mesquite followed suit only in the opposite direction.

Aspen took a running jump and launched herself into

the air, flapping her wings hard to gain some altitude and speed. She knew that they needed to track down and free the lynx mother before something terrible happened.

After fifteen minutes of tromping through the woodland, Sequoia came across a hollow log rotting away amongst a clump of ferns. He could easily smell its inhabitant was inside, perhaps asleep.

"Excuse m-m-me, Mr. Skunk," Sequoia said softly and as politely as he could muster. He didn't want to scare the creature and he most certainly didn't want to get sprayed by its powerful musky glands. He kept at a safe distance just in case.

"Mr. Skunk, sir, m-m-my friends and I are looking for a human that maybe c-c-came this way – a red-eyed man carrying a lynx. Have y-y-you seen or heard him?" Sequoia asked.

After a few seconds and the rustling of dried leaves and twigs, a small black and white striped mammal poked its head out from the end of the log and glanced around. He finally saw Sequoia and after realizing that a curious bear cub didn't pose much of a threat, offered up his answer, "Not me, friend. I been nappin' away in here for quite a bit now. Didn't see a thing. Sorry."

"Okay, th-th-thank you anyway," Sequoia replied, rather disappointed.

The skunk gave some advice to the inquisitive bear: "There's a deer herd that watches these parts pretty

closely, though. If you can find them, I'll bet you get your answer."

That brightened Sequoia's spirits some. "Okay!" he exclaimed. "Thanks again!" The cub sprang off through the underbrush to find the others or perhaps the deer herd if he got lucky.

Mesquite wasn't having any success. The only animal he could find was a mole chomping down on a long, fat earthworm. Being almost completely blind, the mole was no help whatsoever.

Aspen had come across a few birds in the treetops and while they were friendly and quite talkative, they hadn't seen nor heard anything that resembled what she described.

Feeling frazzled, she decided to glide over to a large pine tree that offered a pretty good view of the area. Maybe she could spot her quarry from a better vantage point. In less than a minute after landing on the tree's most protruding limb, Aspen noticed movement below. It was a small herd of deer, perhaps five or six of them, trotting through the woods. They were clearly startled by something.

Aspen hopped off the tree and soared as best she could down toward them. She came to rest on a tall sapling in front of the oncoming deer that were already slowing down to a walking pace, apparently having out-distanced whatever spooked them in the first place.

As the lead deer, a young buck, approached, Aspen spoke up. "Pardon me, young stag," she said in the most composed tone she could muster. "What is it that startled you?" She was hoping the answer would be a perfect description of the hunter.

The buck's ears rotated toward Aspen and he looked back at his herd to ensure they were safe before replying. "Some stupid bear cub is trampling through the forest like an idiot back there," the stubby horned deer said. "He's making all kinds of noise."

Aspen rolled her eyes. "So much for finding witnesses to the whereabouts of the elusive man," she thought to herself.

As the last of the young girl deer gathered around the buck, he made an interesting statement as he started to move on. "If that clown doesn't keep quiet, he's gonna get himself caught by the human."

Aspen's eyes popped wide open. "Human? What human? Have you seen a human around here?"

The boy deer had never met such a curious bird. "Yeah, big guy, too. Looks like he captured a bobcat from what I could tell," he said.

"I think it was a lynx," one of the other deer spoke up.

"Which way did he go?" Aspen asked excitedly.

In unison, the whole herd turned their heads to the west. "That way," they said.

"Less than two miles from here," a large doe with big

brown eyes added, "He's got a large campsite set up, a bunch of helpers with weapons and everything."

"You better be careful, bird," the buck warned as he started to walk away, his tail flicking upward to reveal a large patch of white hair underneath. "That man is trouble. None of us are safe with him around."

Aspen took flight in the direction of her friends. In a short time, she spotted Mesquite, who had already hooked up with Sequoia, and flew down toward them.

"Guys!" she gushed loudly. "We're back in business! The hunter headed west back to his campsite. We got him now!"

Nearly seven miles away in the direction of the Canadian border, Cedar and Juniper had gotten the lynx youngsters out of the iron-ore mine and were headed north again.

But not before Cedar put a plan of his own into play to deal with the threat of the hidden nuclear arsenal. He would need the mother cat reunited with her kits to bring his plan to fruition. He hoped that his teammates had found and freed the captured mother lynx and that she was already racing back to be with her family.

Secretly, Cedar also longed for a chance to take on the red-eyed man himself to dole out his own form of punishment and perhaps turn the hunter into the hunted.

From a hidden spot in a thicket cloaked in the shadow of a tall evergreen, Aspen, Mesquite and Sequoia had a perfect view of Colonel Shaka's camp.

The campsite had two large tents and one extra-large tent aligned at the edge of a clearing and tucked up against a throng of tall conifers. The shelters were made of a lightweight, high-tech material imbued with an elaborate digital camouflage pattern. Rolled up windows and doors allowed for air circulation while dark charcoal mesh material kept mosquitoes and other creatures from slipping in. The tents were staked down at all four corners by nylon cords tied to metal pickets that kept the frames taut and allowed for a flexible yet rigid structure.

A soft, artificial hum emanated from the tent on the far end. Inside, an Axxes-designed generator was steadily providing enough power for Shaka's computer, communications and sophisticated hunting equipment as well as for the Soldierjack recharging station that was used by the robots once their internal energy sources drained at the end of the day.

The generator itself ran on a highly volatile concentrated blend of jet fuel and nitroglycerin. It produced massive amounts of voltage and ran almost silently.

Colonel Shaka himself worked with the scientists in the Axxes labs to create the one-of-a-kind device that would meet his demanding standards but never that of the government due to its unsafe, unstable engine. It was a self-contained power station the size of an office desk that went along on most of Colonel Shaka's missions.

The next tent over, the extra large one, was teeming with activity. It was the operations center and housed the radio and monitoring equipment as well as additional supplies. This shelter also served as Colonel Shaka's quarters with his cot and all his personal gear arranged on the northern end. Soldierjacks came and went from it on a regular basis.

The last tent housed the cages that were set up for Shaka's quarry. Several stacked medium-sized metal dog pens filled most of this shelter and additional containers loaded with extra traps and devices filled up the rest. Inside, the black lynx mother was pacing back and forth in the aluminum crate she was thrown in once Shaka made it back to base camp less than an hour ago. She was not happy.

From their hiding spot overlooking the camp, Mesquite thought he could hear the lynx growling from inside one of the tents. It was an angry, guttural snarl made up of equal portions of rage, fear and sorrow. And definitely feline.

"She's in there, guys," Mesquite said to Sequoia and

Aspen. "I can hear her. She wants out."

Sequoia thrust his snout in the air and sniffed the air for confirmation. "Yeah, she-she-she's in there alright," he said, frustrated.

"At least she's alive and at least we found her," Aspen stated.

"Let's go bust her out!" Mesquite declared and started to move forward.

"Wait!" Aspen interjected, stopping the wolf pup in his tracks. "We need a plan. If we just go bursting in there, we could make things worse."

"Worse? How?" Mesquite shot back.

"Well, we could end up getting captured and tossed in a cage ourselves. Then we're all stuck," Aspen said defiantly.

"I d-d-don't want to get caged, Mesquite," Sequoia said. "I hate cages."

"Okay, fine," Mesquite reluctantly agreed. He paused for a few seconds as he and the others looked the site over rather thoroughly. "I bet we can sneak in there, break her out of her cage and disappear back into the woods."

"Yeah, let's do that!" Sequoia proclaimed.

"Okay, good," said Aspen. "I think we can do this but we're going to need to distract the hunter-man if he's in there as well as all those robots he's got running around."

"I agree," Mesquite said.

"Yeah, me too," Sequoia added.

"Okay, we can do this," Aspen said. "Here's the plan...."

Inside his tent, Colonel Shaka was sitting at his field desk and typing away on his laptop computer. He was emailing digital photos he had just taken of the caged black lynx to a business acquaintance in the Middle East. His wealthy Arab friend was very interested in rare animals and wanted proof of their existence before he would even discuss prices. Shaka knew he could fetch around a million dollars for the whole lynx family. He did not care what happened to the cats once they got there.

As he was writing his offer, a new window popped up on his screen. It was an incoming live video transmission from Nathan Axxes. Shaka quickly closed his communication to his overseas partner and gave Nathan his undivided attention.

"Report!" Axxes screamed into the camera on his end of the video teleconference. He was in his high-rise office in Los Angeles. He, as usual, was angry.

"Good to see you, Mr. Axxes," the Colonel replied with a calm coolness. Shaka wasn't easily intimidated. "I was getting ready to send you some photos of the first cat I've captured. Feisty one, she is."

Axxes gnarled through clenched teeth, "Do not toy with me, Colonel. I am not a patient man."

"No, sir," Shaka said. "I respect that about you."

"So it is true; these black lynxes do exist," Mr. Axxes seethed.

"Oh, indeed they do," his sinister hired hand stated. "Black as coal."

"How long until you can police them all up?" Axxes wanted to know.

"Hard to say," Shaka replied. "This mum I captured recently had a litter. I would judge she has two, maybe three, little ones. Figure I'll bag the babes in a day, maybe two. And then there's the issue about the sire...."

Nathan leaned closer to the web-cam housed inside his laptop in order to emphasize his next statements. "Colonel Shaka, allow me to stress the importance of your little expedition up there. Perhaps I neglected to give you all the details...

"You see, some unimportant little family vacationing from their unimportant little lives happened across these coal-black cats of yours and can't wait to tell the whole world about their little discovery."

Nathan's face was growing redder and his neck rippled with swollen veins at the surface.

"Now, if word gets out that these creatures are indeed alive, half the tree huggers in the world and all the underpaid, self-righteous wildlife officials will scour that property you're stomping all over–and my neighboring property as well–to try to prove the existence of the black lynx," Axxes explained, his words lathered in hatred.

Axxes took a deep breath through his nose, leaned back in his chair and reached for his drink. Colonel Shaka knew not to interrupt and waited for him to finish. It wasn't often that Mr. Axxes told him all the details of his

secret missions, so he eagerly waited to hear his boss' motive behind the eradication of these animals.

"My dear Colonel," Axxes continued more calmly but still with plenty of venom in his voice. "No less than five miles from where you are right now is an old iron-ore mine I've owned for decades. It is closed now, of course, since the area was stolen away from us by the legislature in 1975 and turned into yet another national park that this country really doesn't need."

Colonel Shaka reached next to him and grabbed his canteen. He spun off the cap, took a giant swig and set it back down. He liked where this conversation was going.

"Right around this same time," Nathan continued, "the Axxes organization landed a multi-million-dollar contract to dismantle and destroy a sizable portion of America's old nuclear missile arsenal. It was all part of the nuclear arms pact that turned presidents into pansies.

"Surely you understand how I couldn't pass on an opportunity like this to keep a couple of these for myself. With some trickery, a few harmless decoys and some steep bribes, my gamble paid off. I had snuck two nuclear warheads out from under the noses of the Air Force."

Colonel Shaka was impressed. "So, you kept them this whole time? Pardon my curiousity, sir, but what were you going to do with them?" he asked.

"I wasn't as valiant or as wealthy back in those days, of course, Colonel," the ruthless billionaire said. "So I brokered a deal with a certain disgruntled European country

to smuggle them out on a houseboat through the boundary waters, up into Canada, and on board some tractor trailers they had waiting."

Nathan was actually beaming with pride over his accomplishment. To him, it was a fond memory.

"Anyway," he continued, "we got the nukes moved all the way up there where you are now and hid them away in my old mine as we waited for the exchange with my foreign friends. But they never came. Someone with a loose tongue in their organization said one thing too many and the next thing you know, my business partners were arrested by international police and thrown in a Canadian jail. Fortunately for me, they somehow mysteriously died in custody before they even had the chance to confess or drop any names. Poisoned, I think...."

Shaka nervously chuckled quietly at Nathan's last comment. He was always amazed at the depth of his employer's evilness.

Nathan paused for dramatic effect and to let his last statement become completely absorbed by his huntsman-for-hire. He was trying to be subtle but he also wanted to make it clear that secrets follow you to the grave in his organization.

Mr. Axxes gulped down the last of his beverage and slipped a small ice cube into his mouth, holding it with his tongue as he sucked on it. Once it melted away, he finished his conversation. "So for over thirty years, I've had my own little cache of nuclear weapons. In today's heated

political climate, those things will fetch a hundred times more than my original selling price all those years ago.

"It's a great and powerful feeling having them, Colonel. Very presidential. Godlike even.

"But I digress. Let me get you caught up. You see, a short time ago, I sent some rather rough fellows up there to where you are to, ah, influence the previously mentioned insignificant vacationing family and haven't heard back from them yet. I can only assume something has gone horribly wrong."

Nathan's tone suddenly turned cold and menacing. "Colonel Shaka, it is imperative that you complete your mission there as fast as you can. Employ all means necessary. Burn those lynxes out of there if you have to. Time is of the essence. Do you understand?" Nathan asked.

"Of course, sir," the dark colonel said. "I won't let you down, Mr. Axxes."

"That's good, Colonel," came the reply. "My little secret must be kept at all costs. Make me proud, Colonel Shaka. Don't make me do something I don't want to do."

"I'm on it, sir!" Shaka proclaimed. With a wicked smile, Nathan Axxes terminated the videoconference.

Mesquite, Sequoia and Aspen had made their way undetected down to the tall conifer trees just a few yards behind the camp. They were ready to deploy Aspen's plan and spring the mother lynx from her cage.

From their vantage point it was obvious which tent the captured animal was in, which one housed the generator and where all the bad guys were. They looked each other in the eyes and moved out.

Sequoia bounded over to the tent on the far end that housed the generator. Cautiously, he slid around the tree trunks as he inched his way closer and closer. Finally, he was just a short burst away from his target.

The portly bear cub hunkered down at the edge of where the clearing met the tree grove, paused for a few seconds as he looked left and right, and, after determining that the coast was clear, bolted for the back of the tent. He made it unnoticed.

Aspen, perched on a branch of the tree above Mesquite, watched the whole thing. When she saw Sequoia was in position she called down to her young wolf friend twenty feet below her, "He's safe and ready to go! Now it's your turn!"

Mesquite darted out from the safety of the shadows.

He ran as quickly as his four legs would take him, darting from tree to tree, moving ever closer to take up his planned position behind the largest tent. In less than a minute, he too was safely in place.

Aspen flew from her perch and circled around over Sequoia. She signaled to him that everyone was ready and that it was time to move into the second phase of the operation. Then she continued around on her flight path and cruised past the front of the tents until finally coming to a landing on top of the tent housing the lynx.

Sequoia crept along the backside of the first tent. He carefully peeked around the corner and then snuck around as he headed toward the front. After reaching the next corner, his anxiety grew much stronger. He was just three feet from the front door to the tent now.

Being so close, his nose was overwhelmed by the scent of the strange exhaust the generator inside was emitting. Sequoia's paws quivered underneath him from the vibration the machine was producing and his fur reacted to the electrical charge pulsating outward from the device.

It was nearly unbearable for him. He shook his head to clear his thoughts and try to break, at least temporarily, the physical interference that was overtaking his senses.

He pushed on and moved forward, took a step and turned the corner. He could see a large contraption had been set up in front of the tent. It was a fairly large

metal box with a large radar-like dish attached to the top that pointed up toward the sky. Cables and wires ran all around it like black spaghetti. One extra-large thick, black cable dropped down from the back of it and meandered along the ground back inside the tent. It was no doubt the main power supply.

Sequoia took another step closer, moving ever so slowly as to not arouse any attention.

All of a sudden, a Soldierjack stepped out from inside the tent. The intimidating worker drone was mere inches away from Sequoia. The machine-man turned to his left, not even noticing the crouching bear cub by its right knee, and strode over to the portable satellite dish. The robot entered some data into the system's keyboard and then stood and walked over to the tent in the middle of the small compound.

Sequoia, frozen in mid-step next to the doorway, made his move and scrambled inside the tent with the generator.

The interior of the tent was agonizing. Sequoia's body was flooded with the effects of the mechanical energy radiating from the contraption. Without the tent's metallic-lined walls to offer at least some buffered protection, the little bear was fully exposed to its effects.

But he had to focus. He had a mission.

The generator took up most of the space inside. Cables snaked all about the ground as they ran power

out to other devices within the campsite. Fuel containers were stacked along the far side of the tent. Sequoia knew what he had to do.

Just a few yards away, Mesquite was busy grinding his teeth on the nylon cord connecting one of the rear corners of the main tent to the designated stake for it that was driven deep into the ground. In short order, his sharp little canines had torn through the material and the cord broke free from its anchor. The tent barely flinched as the three remaining ropes took up the slack.

Glancing around, he dashed over to the other corner on the backside of the tent and gnawed through the binding line attached there. It was hard work but his jaws were pretty strong—no doubt strengthened by hours of his favorite pastime of chewing on discarded bones and dropped antlers.

After the second line snapped, Mesquite stealthily moved up toward the front of the main tent. If he could cut just one more line, the whole tent would collapse. It was already starting to buckle. He had to move quickly before anyone inside noticed.

Meanwhile, Aspen had fluttered down to the front of the tent holding the mother lynx. Using her beak, she pulled up on the door flap's zipper enough to slip inside without being noticed.

The lynx was in one of six metal pens stacked on top of one another. She stopped her frantic pacing as soon

as she saw the tiny peregrine falcon hop inside. "Get out of here, bird!" she hissed. "Or you'll find yourself locked in a cage too!"

"I'm here to get you out!" Aspen replied. "Your kits are safe and headed north with friends of mine."

Immediately, the lynx mother's face changed from bitter anger to genuine concern. "My babies...," she whispered apprehensively.

"Don't worry. You'll be back with them in no time," Aspen assured her as she flew up onto the cage next to hers. Peering over the edge, Aspen studied the cage holding the lynx to see how to get it open.

The door to her pen was locked shut by a hinged D-ring like the kind used by mountain climbers, hikers and the military. The hinges were self-contained units and the rest of the cage was fully welded.

Aspen quickly realized she would have to undo the D-ring, so she flittered down and landed on the door. Grasping tightly with her talons, and feeling like a performing parrot, she clung to the bars on the door and moved into position over the metal clasp.

The mother lynx watched as Aspen clutched one side of the D-ring in her beak and the other side with one foot. Defying gravity with bursts from her wings, Aspen managed to close the clasp onto itself and lift it up and out of the connecting holes in the cage. She dropped it to the ground once it was clear.

The wildcat immediately leaped out of her prison cell and landed softly on her four enormous paws. She was headed straight for the door of the tent.

"Wait!" Aspen shouted. "You don't want to get shot trying to escape! My friends are here – wait for their diversion!"

The lynx looked at Aspen with wild, yellow eyes. "What diversion?" she asked with pronounced overtones of disbelief and amazement in her voice.

Suddenly, an explosion rocked the compound. The ear-shattering eruption shook the ground and the trees shuddered against the abrupt concussion. A huge plume of smoke rose up from the tent housing the generator.

Sequoia came running up to the tent that the lynx and Aspen were peeking out of. "Let's go! Let's go!" he shouted, his ears still ringing from the blast.

The little bear had tipped over several of the fuel cells piled up next to the generator. Once the leaking liquid touched the hot exhaust of the machine, it caught fire and erupted like a man-made volcano. Smoldering pieces were still raining down all around.

Colonel Shaka, who had just gotten back online with his exotic animal buyers, was in the middle of his valuable transaction when the explosion occurred. It knocked him completely off his chair and sent his laptop sprawling across the room.

Furious, he leaped back to his feet. "Find out what's

going on! Control the damage! Put out the fire!" he screamed to the Soldierjacks surrounding him.

Not trusting the explosion to some random accident, Shaka staggered over to his cot and grabbed his gear and weapons while the Soldierjacks under his command scrambled for the door.

Then, without notice, the whole tent buckled and collapsed on top of their heads. Mesquite had cut the third support line at the perfect moment. Confused and blinded within the folds of the tent, the Soldierjacks tripped and fell over each other.

Regrouped, the three Natural Forces members and their newly sprung prisoner escaped from the chaos. They fled out across the clearing, headed for the forest on the other side, with the mother lynx leading the way.

Colonel Shaka, boiling with rage, pulled out his huge Bowie knife, tore through the tent material covering him and rose up out of the giant slit he had cut in the turmoil-filled deflated tent.

Looking around, he could see the tent that held the generator inside was completely destroyed from the explosion and what remained was still burning. The blast had damaged the satellite dish and the communications equipment beyond repair. The largest piece of the custom generator that was even recognizable was not much larger than a four-slice toaster.

To his left, he noticed that the door to the tent that

housed his captured trophy was left wide open. She had escaped.

With his right hand, Colonel Shaka flipped up the red alloy patch that covered his artificial eye. The sophisticated lenses within his restored eye socket digitally scanned the area and caught a glimpse of movement across the field in front of him. The heat signatures of three animals and a bird were tracked by Shaka's telescoping implant as they hightailed it away from his destroyed encampment. Optically zooming across the distance verified that one of them was his black lynx.

"No!" Colonel Shaka screamed. His roar, bellowed up from deep within his huge chest cavity, was so loud that the escaping animals actually paused to look back. "No! No! No!" echoed across the valley. Shaka was furious. And he was about to go on the warpath.

"You cannot escape from me!" Shaka yelled across the valley. Then he used his big right hand to enter a combination of keystrokes on the metal band wrapped around his left wrist.

Instantly, in response to Shaka's wireless commands, a series of devices surrounding his campsite initiated. In a quick, clock-like sweeping motion, four rows of parallel red laser beams suddenly turned on and encircled the entire perimeter. In the blink of an eye, the clever Colonel had trapped his prey inside a giant fence line.

The lynx slid to a halt just inches from the deadly laser beams, followed closely behind by Mesquite, Sequoia and Aspen.

"Oh, great!" Mesquite exclaimed. "This guy's good!"

Aspen flew up higher to look around. She could clearly see the laser-fence had them closed in completely. The lowest beam was too low to crawl under and the top one was too tall to jump over. "It's not lookin' good, boys!" she hollered. "I can fly over this, but you all are in big trouble."

"I can't believe this!" the mother lynx shrieked. "Who is this guy? Why won't he leave me alone?"

Across the field, the Soldierjacks had finally gotten out from under the collapsed tent. The colonel ordered

two of them to stay behind with him to put out the fire from the explosion and he sent the other eight after his quarry.

The Soldierjacks were running across the open land at full speed, armed with orders to kill and clutching their trusty Flamesaws – half chainsaw, half flamethrower tools the Axxes drones used with brutal efficiency for clearing forests.

"We're dead now," the lynx muttered.

Three blinding bursts of blue light erupted around the mother lynx, emanating from Aspen, Mesquite and Sequoia as their amulets sensed imminent danger and triggered their metamorphosis.

The startled lynx cowered from fright as she watched her new friends unexpectedly turn into super-sized, super-powered beings right before her eyes.

Mesquite barked out his commands: "Aspen! Sequoia and I will engage and stall these robots long enough for you to fly the lynx over the fence line. Once she's safely on the other side and heading for home, come join us in the fight! I got a feeling we're going to have our hands full!"

"On it!" Aspen decreed. With a few powerful strokes from her giant wings, the peregrine falcon-turned-warrior shot straight up and then turned for a high-speed dive.

"Hold still, lynx momma!" Aspen cried down from the skies to the astounded wildcat. "I'll have you clear in no time!"

Aspen tucked her wings against her body and shot straight down like a spear from the heavens. As she got near the lynx, she pulled up, swung her legs forward and carefully snatched the black cat in her talon-feet. Then, without losing momentum, she continued on her aerial arc until she was headed out and over the nearest laser fence.

"Don't be scared," Aspen said to her. "Run as fast as you can for the border. You'll find your children by the tallest tree on the highest hill."

The mother lynx was in total shock. She could not believe what she was seeing. As soon as Aspen set her down safely on the other side, the rare black lynx snapped out of it and took off running at full speed.

As the black lynx was sprinting for home, Sequoia and Mesquite were clashing head-on with the oncoming squad of Soldierjack robots.

Horrendous plumes of fire shot forth from the Soldierjack's Flamesaws but were deflected harmlessly away with Sequoia's mighty magical shield. As the giant grizzly moved ever closer, he reached out with his massive right hand and grabbed one of the robots that had gotten too close.

Crushing the machine-man's head in his steely grip, Sequoia then whipped the Soldierjack's body around and flung it smashing against two others who didn't have time to move out of the way.

Mesquite leaped into action and launched himself into the air using his spear shaft as a pole vault. The man-wolf propelled himself up and over a Soldierjack who had just fired a blazing stream of fire where Mesquite had just been.

Landing behind the android, Mesquite dropped it to the ground with a hard kick to the knee joint and then drove his spear deep into its chest. The robot spasmed and bucked and eventually shut down altogether.

Another Soldierjack ran up to Mesquite and swung the ripping blade of its Flamesaw right at the warrior-wolf's head.

Mesquite rolled just in time and the chainsaw blade swiped at thin air, missing its intended target by less than an inch.

The superhuman wolf sprang to his feet and in one lethal motion, swung his spear around and struck the Soldierjack hard on the side of its head. The robot's neck nearly snapped, but it recoiled and brought its Flamesaw around for another slashing blow.

Mesquite managed to dodge the attack again and heaved himself up into a spinning kick that landed with brute force to the Soldierjack's faceplate. This time the robot's neck nearly separated completely from its body as its head snapped backward so far that it touched its own steel spine. Mesquite finished the wobbly-headed robot with one final punch to the midsection. It collapsed

to the ground motionless.

Meanwhile, Sequoia found himself surrounded by the final three Soldierjacks who readied their Flamesaws for a fiery finish to the heroic grizzly. He knew he couldn't deflect all three flamethrowers.

Just as he was about to call for help, a barrage of turquoise-colored streaks shot down from the sky and exploded against two of the Soldierjacks.

Aspen had arrived on the scene and let loose with her ballistic feather-missiles that were mystically charged and deadly accurate. Like glowing blue meteorites, Aspen's projectiles impacted hard on-target and knocked both Soldierjacks to the ground and permanently out of commission.

Sequoia smashed his shield against the last remaining Soldierjack who was no match for his power and ferocity. The robot buckled under the blow and fell to its demise in a heap of bent metal and a cascade of sparks.

Across the field, Colonel Shaka watched the whole thing. He was truly impressed. Finally, he had animals worthy of fighting. He hoped this would be his greatest challenge yet.

Shaka strode confidently across the clearing. He was now fully armed – gear and equipment were strapped all over him.

Assessing the three warriors amongst the carnage of destroyed Soldierjacks, he determined that Aspen was

the greatest immediate threat. With her long-distance unlimited supply of weapons and ruthless aerial attack, not to mention her amazing speed, Shaka realized that the heroic falcon must be brought down immediately.

Ironically, it was she who noticed him first. Aspen called to her teammates, "Here comes a live one, guys! Looks like the red-eyed hunter himself wants to learn a lesson too!"

She swooped up and positioned herself for an assault.

"Aspen!" Mesquite called out. "Hold up! We don't know what this guy's capable of!" His words went unheeded. Aspen was already engaged in combat.

She dove and flipped her torso – whipping her right wing around and sending a volley of explosive feathers streaking at the huntsman.

Colonel Shaka lurched his athletic frame out of the way and barely avoided her destructive barrage that exploded in rapid sequence on the ground.

Shaka turned and pulled out a large high-tech alloy boomerang attached to the back of his armored vest and touched a button on its base. Activated, the curved weapon hummed as he whipped it at Aspen who was soaring above the battlefield.

"Oh, please," Aspen yelled in her animal language as she dipped rather easily to dodge the silver device. "You're going to have to do a lot better than that!"

Watching from below, Shaka smiled as the boomerang

whirled past her with incredible speed. It slowed a little as it reached its return point and then shot back on its return path. Aspen hadn't experienced a boomerang before and wasn't ready for the backlash.

"Aspen! Look out behind you!" Sequoia roared just a second too late.

A few feet before impact, the boomerang's bent metal arms opened up at a hidden hinge in the center to form a rounded x-shape. The alloy weapon slammed against Aspen's back and the opened arms snapped shut around her shoulders and torso while releasing a powerful electrical burst. Unconscious and bound in a metal harness, Aspen fell hard to the earth.

Shaka smiled and snarled at his latest conquest. "I've downed several condors with that very weapon, missy," he shouted to the unaware bird-lady. "Glad to make you its latest victim!"

Mesquite and Sequoia watched in horror as their female friend hit the ground. They surged after the hunter with vengeance on their mind. Surely one man, no matter how well armed or enhanced, wouldn't stand a chance against both a super-powered bear and a wolf.

Shaka readied for their attack. He swung out a bazooka style of weapon from his back and aimed it at the giant bear.

Sequoia brought up his shield just as Shaka fired. A hefty football-shaped missile with a trail of smoke pouring

out behind it shot from the rocket launcher directly at the grizzly and slammed against his shield.

It was just as Shaka planned. He was the self-proclaimed world's most lethal hunter because he studied his prey. He knew just what they would do and exactly what they were capable of. Shaka was a genius at exploiting any weakness and finding a way to win.

The oblong rocket smashed against Sequoia's shield and released its precious cargo. Like an attacking giant octopus, a huge net made of titanium sprang out from inside the missile on impact and enveloped the colossal grizzly – shield and all. Laced with neuro-toxins, the net immediately paralyzed the giant bruin. Sequoia fell helpless in the dirt, wrapped tightly in the metallic lacework that was his undoing.

"Works great against charging rhinos, too," Shaka growled with a wide grin. He was truly in his element.

Mesquite had closed the distance for close combat. He lunged at Colonel Shaka who ducked the attack while tossing his spent bazooka to the ground.

Both warriors spun to face each other. Equal in size, hand-to-hand combat would determine who was the more experienced fighter and better adversary.

Mesquite bared his fangs and summoned up an icy growl. His fists were clenched tight around his spear and he squatted for an assault.

Shaka pulled the custom-designed whip off his belt

and unfurled it above his head. He let loose with a horrific snap of the alloy lash directly at Mesquite's face.

The wolf-warrior managed to bring up his spear shaft as the crack of the whip pierced the air. The whip coiled tightly around his spear and, with unexpected strength, Shaka yanked it right out from Mesquite's hands.

"Let's see you fight without your weapons, wolf-man!" Shaka blared.

"I'd like to see you do the same, red-eye!" Mesquite retorted but Shaka only heard the snarling of a wolf.

Mesquite lunged to the ground and brought up one leg for a well-placed kick to Shaka's gut. The South African exhaled abruptly as he fell backward and dropped his whip, but he rolled with the blow and somehow landed back on his feet.

He held his stomach with one hand as he pulled out three small black orbs with the other from his vest pocket. Shaka whipped the ebony balls at Mesquite that detonated on contact against the wolf's chest and knocked Mesquite to the ground in a cloud of smoke and dust.

Coughing, Mesquite got up again and looked around but Shaka was nowhere to be seen. Suddenly, the whip was around Mesquite's throat. With amazing speed, Shaka had snuck up behind him and managed to wrap the alloy bullwhip around his neck. It was excruciating and made it impossible to breathe.

"I could just choke you to death, beast!" the colonel

shouted to the hero in his clutches. "But you three are far too valuable to kill just yet!"

With that, the colonel pushed a hidden button on the handle of the whip that sent a powerful jolt down the line and knocked Mesquite completely out.

In a matter of minutes, Colonel Shaka had defeated all three of the Natural Forces. His blood was pumping with adrenaline and his chest was heaving from exertion. To him, it was his most glorious day.

Maneuvering two temporarily motherless and constantly fussing black lynx kittens around lush northern forestland saturated with lakes and rivers was proving to be a stressful task indeed for Juniper and Cedar.

The foursome was exhausted. Hurdling logs and creeks were bad enough for a young badger and a small ferret, but making a pair of wildcat babies do the same took all the energy and patience they had.

But they kept pushing on and making progress, ever northward. Mosquito swarms and inquisitive large birds-of-prey were constant annoyances. The shadowy, leafy undergrowth offered relief from most of their troubles and provided a much cooler temperature at the same time.

Cedar had about all he could take. His already limited amount of patience had been taxed to the limit. "If I hear either one of you two ask if we're there yet just one more time," Cedar grumbled, "I swear I will throw you both in the nearest lake."

"Cedar!" Juniper exclaimed, shocked at his thinly veiled threat posed to the youngsters, "That is no way to talk!"

She turned to face them – their awestruck faces hinted that they were about to burst into fits of crying – and Juniper knew that would probably be all Cedar

could handle. "Now don't worry about Uncle Cedar," she said, trying to reassure the little cats, "he's going to take good care of you and he would never ever do anything to hurt you."

Then she turned her attention to her brash badger colleague and scowled at him as best she could before putting him on the spot. "Isn't that right, Cedar?"

The tuft-eared, big-pawed feline youngsters stopped in their tracks and slowly turned around in unison to hear from the grumpy badger himself.

Seeing their big, sad blue eyes desperate for a reassuring answer, Cedar gave them the answer they wanted to hear whether he meant it or not. "Yeah," he replied, but with very little feeling, "what she said. Now let's keep moving."

The little group continued plodding along, their feet muddied and sore. They were less than ten miles from the Canadian border.

The sudden sound of an onrushing creature startled Cedar who was in the rear of the column to protect the most vulnerable spot. He spun to face the rapidly advancing animal with teeth bared and claws extended.

The tall wild grass weaved and parted as the animal came bursting through and nearly smashed head-on with the defensive badger cub. It was a black lynx. It was the mother.

She recognized Cedar instantly – after all, he was the

only badger in the world with a turquoise medallion hanging from his neck. She was panting profusely.

She could barely speak. "My children," she managed to gasp. "Where are my children?"

Cedar, relaxed now after recognizing her, didn't have to reply. The lynx kits poured over him to get to their mother.

"Momma! Momma!" they screamed with excitement. "Never leave us again, Momma!"

Tears streamed down her charcoal face. "I won't, my babies. I won't."

Juniper and Cedar could see the big cat had been running for a long time. Her fur was tattered—raked by passing branches and thorns, her feet were blistered and bloody. Foam was caked in the corners of her mouth. She was exhausted.

For a long while she just lay there, on her back, rolling around with her kittens jumping all over her, licking her face and pouncing on her chest. She was frazzled and worn out, but reuniting with her little ones eclipsed her exhaustion at least for a few short minutes.

Juniper and Cedar left the lynxes alone as they scanned the distance, and the sky, for the return of their teammates. Seeing nothing, and feeling as if something was wrong, Juniper interrupted the wildcat reunion, "I'm sorry, but are our friends far behind? Did they follow you back?"

The mother lynx suddenly turned somber. She pulled

herself back up to her feet and looked in the direction from where she came. Her kits were still vying for her attention.

"Be still now, children," she told them. Then she turned to Juniper and Cedar who sat idly nearby, hoping for an answer they wouldn't dread. "Your friends; the bear, the wolf and the falcon, they came and rescued me from the red-eyed hunter and his soldiers. We were escaping from his camp when suddenly he had us trapped again. But they, they..." the female black lynx was having a hard time relaying what she saw, "...they changed into, into, more powerful versions of themselves and then the bird, Aspen, flew me away to safety."

The lynx felt like she was telling the details of a dream. It didn't seem real, but it was. Her babies sat watching and listening in wonder. They were captivated by their mother's story of being rescued by super-powered animals. Then she noticed the amulets hanging from the necks of Juniper and Cedar and realized they probably had the same capabilities as their missing friends.

"I took off running, to get back to my little ones, but I could hear your friends in battle behind me," she said. "It was fierce and fast. When I got to a little clearing on a hilltop, I turned and looked back. They had beaten the hunter's soldiers, but then he came after them. He is a very dangerous man. He threw something at Aspen and knocked her out of the sky.

"I almost ran back to try to help, but I knew I couldn't – the fence was too tall to jump. I was scared for them. The big one, Sequoia, he went down next. And then it was the wolf's turn… I thought he might do it, you know, beat the mean man, but he couldn't. I was scared. I ran as fast as I could back here. To my babies… and to warn you."

Cedar snarled and Juniper stiffened. This was not the news they wanted to hear. They had to save their friends.

The lynx continued as her kids tucked up against her, frightened. Her story was scaring them. "You cannot beat this man. His weapons are too powerful. His heart is as black as my fur. You should run away to the north with us. I fear it is too late for your friends."

"Never!" Cedar snapped. His amulet was already starting to glow. "No! We stick to the plan."

Juniper, herself on the cusp of morphing into her super-self, chided in, "There is more at stake here than you know about. There is a cave a few miles back that is hiding nuclear warheads. This is all connected somehow. You and your kittens have an important role that you must carry out. We will go back and fight the hunter and free our friends. Can we count on you?"

The lynx was astonished. She just wanted things to be the way it used to be. But she also owed these five strange creatures her very life. "Yes, you can count on us. Tell me what you need us to do."

In short order, Cedar revealed his plan to the shadow

cats. The lynx, in turn, told them how to find the hunter's campsite. She stressed to them again that they could not win – the red-eyed man was simply too strong.

"Don't worry about us," Cedar assured her as his and Aspen's medallions continued to intensely glow like miniature bright blue suns. "You just do what we asked. We'll take care of the hunter."

Blinded by the exploding turquoise light that enveloped Cedar and Juniper, the black lynxes squinted their eyes as they tried to watch the magical transformation take place before them. The young badger and the little ferret morphed and expanded, tripling in size – changing form into half-human, half-animal super beings. In an instant it was over…two supernatural warriors replaced two earthly mammals in a brilliant blue burst.

Cedar turned to Juniper who was coiling like a spring to take off. "Go! I'll catch up! Stall the hunter until I get there."

In a flash, she was gone. A turquoise streak followed her through the forest as she shot away like a rocket.

Cedar spun to look down at the black lynx family who were staring in disbelief at what they had just witnessed. "Please don't worry about us," he said, his voice was deep, dark and gravel-like. He flexed his huge claws that extended from hands to emphasize his point. "We got this. This guy's going down."

Then he turned and took off running toward his destiny with Colonel Shaka. Cedar is a squat and muscular figure but amazingly light on his feet. In a few seconds, he was also out of sight.

At Shaka's campsite, Sequoia and Mesquite awoke to find themselves bound together and inside one of the Colonel's ring-shaped cages and guarded by two Soldierjacks holding Flamesaws.

In their helpless states, the dark hunter was able to tie them up with an incredibly strong yet thin alloy strand, like super-strength piano wire, that wrapped tightly around them several times. It was ingenious – the more they tried to pull on the wire or to break free, the more it would slice into their skin. Even if they managed to break free, they still would have to deal with the circle of electrically charged, ten-foot-tall steel bars that surrounded them.

Aspen was just a few feet away, stuffed inside one of the larger metal crates. From the door of her pen hung a grenade that was rigged to detonate if anyone messed with the latch. "Glad to see you boys are finally awake," the captured falcon called out to them. "Are you alright?"

"Yeah, sore, but fine," Mesquite groaned. "I can't believe this guy was able to beat us."

Sequoia twisted his head around enough to see Aspen out of the corner of his eye, "Yeah, what did he hit me with? I can still feel its effects. I can barely move."

"What now?" Aspen said.

"We wait," replied Mesquite. "Juniper and Cedar must know something's wrong. And the hunter doesn't know

about them. Hopefully, they'll be here soon."

Colonel Shaka came out from his tent he had recently rebuilt. The fires from the sabotaged generator explosion were extinguished now and he had also ordered the remaining Soldierjacks to remove the remnants of their destroyed robot kin. Their broken bodies were stacked next to the main tent. Shaka didn't like to leave any evidence behind, and he figured he could ship them out once he established communications again with Axxes headquarters and order a truck to come out.

Two Soldierjacks were busily trying to reassemble the damaged satellite radio. The laser fence was turned off again and an assortment of several more traps lay ready to be fielded.

Colonel Shaka heard his captives making noise and wanted to see them again in their conscious state. They were the most amazing animals he had ever encountered. He picked up his rifle and headed out to where the animals were being held – out in the open, in the hot sun.

"Well, well, well," the proud hunter said, assuming they could understand his words. They seemed human enough. "Once again in the classic struggle of man versus beast, man wins, eh?" A pompous smirk was carved across his arrogant face.

Slowly, he strutted past their cages, admiring his latest conquest. He couldn't fathom their origins and was absolutely captivated by them.

"I can see the influence of the American Indian in all of you," he said, coldly. "But what are you? How is it possible that you even exist?"

Mesquite turned, snarling at his captor. His canines were like alabaster icicles.

"Got some fight left in you?" Colonel Shaka teased as he leaned in closer to Mesquite, knowing full well that the wolf-warrior could hardly budge. He stuck the barrel of his rifle through the energized bars, being careful not to accidentally touch them, and forcefully prodded Mesquite in the ribs. "When will you critters learn that when Colonel Shaka comes after you, there is nowhere you can run, nowhere you can hide?"

The huntsman stood up again and strutted over to Aspen who was crammed tightly in her booby-trapped wire caged cell. He glared at her with his one good eye.

"Did you really think you could challenge me?" he chastised. "You are a beautiful creature, bird woman. But no match for me. I am the better species, here. I am the superior being!"

Aspen railed against the side of her crate, but to no avail. It was too cramped and she didn't have room to launch her feather weapons, much less turn over. She relished the thought of scratching his face with her talons.

"Ha! Are you mad at me now? Do you want to fight me again?" Shaka was enjoying this. "Did you think you accomplished anything? I am no fool."

Shaka reached into his vest pocket and pulled out a device about the size of a cell phone. He pulled up on the recessed antenna and turned it on. The screen came to life and a radar-like needle swept across it in a clockwise arc. A red blip appeared in the upper right-hand corner.

"See this?" Shaka asked as he held up the gadget for all to see. He was elated. "I embedded a tracking chip in that cat just before you all arrived. I like to monitor my trophies as I send them overseas to ensure they get there and as a favor to my clients."

Shaka was gloating now. He knew Mr. Axxes would be so pleased with him. And he was going to be rich. He dangled the tracking device in front of Sequoia's bewildered face. "With this device, the black lynx you idiots set free is not only going to be easy to find, but she's going to lead me right to the rest of 'em! You three actually did me a favor!" He finished by taunting them with a raucous, scornful laugh.

A sudden movement whooshed by Shaka and tore the contraption out of his hand. Shaka's eye opened wide as he stared into his empty palm, disbelieving.

Then he looked over to see the thief, a ferret-turned-warrior, standing next to Aspen's cage with the device in her little hand. The four-foot-tall speedster held it above her head and then smashed it down on the corner of Aspen's pen. It shattered into a thousand pieces that splintered all about.

"Juniper!" Aspen, Mesquite and Sequoia exclaimed.

"Thought you guys might miss me," Juniper quipped. "Has this guy been bothering you?"

Colonel Shaka let loose with a horrible, angry roar. That was his only tracking device and was programmed with the transmission code to the chip in the black lynx. He would have to start over. He was furious.

He shouted a curse at the new arrival and brought his rifle up to his shoulder.

"Uh-oh," Juniper said and then took off. She was too fast for even Colonel Shaka's enhanced abilities. He fired again and again at the blue streak but couldn't target her. Bullets kicked up divots in the turf all around Juniper, but she dodged every shot.

After emptying his clip, Shaka threw the rifle at her in disgust. It clattered against the ground and skid to a stop a few feet from her.

"Aw, did I make the big, ugly man angry?" Juniper teased in her animal language for the benefit of her caged comrades.

Shaka unhooked the whip at his side and swung it about over his head as he lined up his assault. Juniper readied for the bullwhip and dived forward as it came crashing down on the spot she had just stood. A harsh crack filled the air and Shaka recoiled his weapon for another strike.

Juniper moved in at full speed, closing the distance

and making the whip less effective. She zoomed under Shaka's legs, turned and ran up his back and then hammered him on the head with a series of ultra-fast punches and kicks.

"Graaah!" Shaka bellowed as he staggered backward, swinging his fist wildly about, trying to hit the impossibly fast attacker.

He didn't get a chance to study the feisty ferret ahead of time. He needed to formulate a plan and select the appropriate weapon.

But Juniper wasn't slowing down. She pulled out her magical hatchets, one in each hand. With their turquoise stone blades glowing brightly, she launched into her attack.

Juniper cruised around her adversary like a tornado, striking away as Shaka protected his head and tucked his exposed areas inside his protective gear as best he could. Juniper's flurry of chops hammered away at his weapons and against his reinforced outfit. Within just a few seconds, she had rendered his sidearm and the bazooka on his back worthless, not to mention the dozens of bruises and contusions she pummeled into him that would remain for weeks.

"Enough!" Shaka screamed from his tucked, cowering position. He desperately reached over and depressed a button on his wristband. Instantaneously, the huge shoulder pads on his hunting vest popped open and two

giant clouds of green smoke sprayed out from both sides, surrounding him in concealing, defensive smog.

Juniper was temporarily blinded. She broke off her attack and stumbled away, coughing and hacking and wiping her eyes. She was feeling dizzy.

Shaka quickly pulled a breathing apparatus out from a hidden pouch. He put it over his nose and mouth and watched as his fast-moving assailant finally collapsed from breathing the knockout gas.

The Colonel rose to his feet and stepped out from the green haze. He was bruised and beaten, but victorious. By skillfully using his tools, he had once again prevailed.

He didn't like this new combatant at all – she was too fast and had inflicted some serious damage to him, his equipment, and his plans. She also had nearly defeated him.

Shaka walked over to Juniper who was laying face first in the dirt. He put one of his huge boots on her back and pulled his Bowie knife out from its sheath. This little warrior had also embarrassed him in front of the other animals and that hurt Shaka the most. He wanted to prove to all of them that he was the ultimate warrior on any continent.

"No!" Aspen and the others shouted as they watched in horror. How ruthless could this man be?

Without warning, the ground behind Colonel Shaka burst open. Cedar emerged from his earthly tunnel just inches behind the hunter-for-hire with a blood-curdling

howl. His claws were pulsating bright blue and his eyes were like smoldering green sapphires. Chunks of dirt and rock fell off his heaving shoulders as he stood there, ready to rip Shaka in half.

Colonel Shaka froze. He could tell the creature behind him was another one of these wretched beasts endowed somehow with superpowers. And this one seemed to be the scariest of all. He could feel Cedar's breath on his neck. Goosebumps covered his flesh, as Shaka crouched over Juniper, terrified for his life.

Slowly, Shaka raised his arms in surrender and dropped his big knife. It fell straight down and embedded itself, blade first, into the ground with a tinny sound. As soon as it did, Shaka somersaulted over Juniper and rolled around to face his newest attacker.

Cedar didn't flinch. He wanted a fair fight. But he wouldn't get one.

"Soldierjacks, to me!" Shaka called out. "Defend your commander!"

Cedar whirled around to face the Soldierjacks who were rushing to engage him. He went on the offensive and ran straight at them. Amongst fiery blasts from the flamethrowers and the roar of the spinning chainsaw blades, Cedar flung himself into the pack of robot soldiers with his claws fully extended.

With the badger hero occupied, Colonel Shaka picked up his knife and retrieved his whip and then scrambled

around the battling Soldierjacks to his tent. He needed to get to his gear.

Cedar was fully engaged, his arms flailing about and tearing into the Soldierjacks. They were no match for his fury and he vented all his anger into destroying them. The sharp eight-inch-long nails of the unreal badger cleaved through the bodies of the uniformed metal drones. From a whirlwind of slicing, shredding ferocity, Cedar finally emerged triumphant.

He looked around to find Colonel Shaka standing alone a few feet from his tent, intently staring back at Cedar. He was holding nothing but his knife in his hand. He signaled at the badger to come over. One on one. Man versus beast.

Cedar jumped at the chance and bounded over wildly at the hunter. Ten massive claws against one huge knife. Cedar liked his odds.

As he got closer, Cedar slowed his approach. Sauntering ever closer, he was looking Shaka up and down, eyeing him for a point of attack. The huntsman strangely didn't seem ready – he wasn't tensing for Cedar's onslaught. It was like he wanted the badger to attack him.

Cedar slowly stepped closer, closing the gap until he was just a few feet in front of him. Suddenly, Cedar's foot stepped onto something buried in the sand. Something metal, something foreign. In an instant, two

bowed metal braces snapped shut on Cedar's leg.

Cedar screamed out in agony as the leg trap slammed shut, it's jagged teeth cutting through his black and white fur and digging into this flesh. He instantly fell to one knee, clutching his leg in agony.

Colonel Shaka moved in for the kill. "None of you can beat me!" the hunter blared. "I am the destroyer of all animals! I am your master and king!"

Mesquite could take no more. "Sequoia! I've got an idea! Get ready!" he said, still tied to his best friend inside their fabricated prison cell.

Relaxing his mind and slowing his heart, Mesquite summoned his inner self. Shutting out the chaos around him, he reflected inside and found his liberation. In a near sleep-like state, Mesquite suddenly shrank back down to his former self. He became a wolf pup again.

Instantly dropping 250 pounds of mass, the wires that once constricted taut around him and Sequoia were suddenly loose. Mesquite easily slipped out from the inflexible coils and moved out of the way to let Sequoia stand up. The mighty grizzly rolled over and lifted the wires over his head, throwing them to the ground.

The activity caught Shaka's eye. He turned his attention away from Cedar. "No!" he shouted. "What are you doing? You can't escape!"

Free from his bonds, Mesquite called for action. "Good! Now toss me out of here!" he blurted to his cellmate.

Sequoia put the pup in his huge mitt and gently tossed him up and over the bars. As Mesquite hurled out of the electrified cage, he transformed once again in mid-air amongst a bombardment of aquamarine-colored

light. By the time he landed, he was fully formed, ready for battle.

Colonel Shaka left Cedar to deal with his snared leg and ran over to engage the escaped wolf. With his whip swirling over his head, crackling with high amounts of energy, the hunter moved in to deliver a lethal blow.

Mesquite was ready for him. He hoisted his mystical spear over his shoulder and flung it at the approaching South African with brutal force. The spear was slightly off target and Shaka simply leaned to his left to allow it to pass by. The mystical lance rocketed past the hunter, its turquoise blue tip shining like the sun.

"Ha! You missed!" the arrogant Colonel blurted as he moved closer into striking distance.

Mesquite stood his ground, smiling.

Behind the Colonel, Mesquite's spear smashed into the control box for the cell he had just escaped from. A perfect throw, the spear smashed the device into oblivion.

Immediately, the bars to Sequoia's prison lost their charge. They were now just ten-foot-tall steel bars and no match for a provoked, aggravated giant grizzly – especially one with superpowers.

With a thunderous roar, Sequoia pulled the bars apart and leaped out of his cell. He stood ready next to Mesquite as their attacker advanced. Two against one.

Shaka's alloy bullwhip came crashing down just as Sequoia's shield came up to absorb its impact. Like a

giant metal cobra, the whip struck faster than the speed of sound and the air cracked like a gunshot to prove it.

With a smooth gesture of his arm, the wicked hunter recalled his weapon for another, faster swat. He was aiming for Mesquite this time.

The wolf-warrior was prepared. As the silver lash came whipping down, Mesquite barely dodged its lightning strike. Shaka's bullwhip struck against the ground like a larger caliber bullet, kicking up a small explosion of dust, dirt and rocks.

Colonel Shaka pulled his whip back again with a flick of his wrist. He twirled it back behind him when suddenly he felt its length was cut short as it came apart just a few feet down the handle.

Shocked, he turned to see the cause of his equipment's malfunction only to find Cedar standing there, claws burning blue and an evil smile stretched across his badger face. The main length of Shaka's specialized whip lay in pieces at the ferocious badger's feet. Cedar had freed himself from the painful steel jaws of the leg trap and snuck up behind the Colonel, shredding his favorite weapon when it was behind his back. Three against one.

Juniper suddenly rushed up at full speed behind her antagonist and swept his left leg out from under him. Shaka crashed hard to the ground, flat on his back. His entire world was collapsing around him. Juniper had fully

recovered and was ready to bring some more punishment against him. Four against one.

Sequoia stepped over to Aspen who was still stuck in her cramped pen. With both hands, he held his shield up over his head and smashed it down on the grenade wired to the door of her crate. The grenade dislodged, pin and all, and fell to the ground, about to detonate. Sequoia quickly covered the baseball-sized bomb with his massive, mystical shield and held it to the ground with all his impressive weight and muscle. From underneath, the grenade exploded, sending shockwaves rippling across the earth for a dozen acres all around.

With her cage door open, Aspen sprung free from her confinement and shot into sky. It felt so good to be able to stretch her wings to full length again. She circled Colonel Shaka from above as her four friends encircled him below. Five against one.

The Axxes assassin struggled back to his feet. Still clutching the three-foot long remnant of his shattered whip in his right hand, Shaka reached up with his left and pulled out his knife. Just as he did, a streak of turquoise shot down from above and blasted the knife out of his hand. Aspen had wanted to do that for quite some time.

With his left hand numb from the explosive sting of Aspen's feather missile, Colonel Shaka knew the end was near. The predator had become the prey. In a last ditch act of quiet desperation, he looked around for some help;

a remaining Soldierjack maybe or perhaps another weapon of his lay just within reach. There was nothing but five angry super-powered animals.

It was Colonel Shaka's last stand. He just stood there, trembling, holding little more than just the handle of his ruptured alloy bullwhip that was spitting electrical sparks out from it like an extra-large sparkler on the Fourth of July.

The Natural Forces slowly circled around him counter-clockwise. With every step, the ring grew tighter.

It looked as if the great hunter was about to cry. His lower lip began to twitch and he dropped down to his knees, hoping for mercy. Without his weapons or sneaky tactics, the fight had completely gone out of him. He was about to be beaten by animals. His greatest fear of all.

But then he thought of something. A way to keep his perfect record...a way out. A crazy look came across his sweaty, dusty face. And a perplexing smile spread across his mouth. On wobbly legs, he rose back to his feet.

"You can't beat me," he said, giggling strangely and glancing around to all five of his native-born conquerors. "Colonel Shaka can't be defeated...especially by animals! You can't beat me, you filthy, hairy, feathery creatures! You can't beat me! I'm Colonel Shaka!"

In amazement, the Natural Forces team watched as the great egomaniacal hunter stuck the voltage-spitting, fractured whip handle directly under his chin. The

jolt threw the big man six feet back where he landed on his head in an unconscious heap. Small wisps of smoke seeped out from under his red metal eye patch. Drool dribbled out of the corner of his mouth and for some reason, his right hand was twitching uncontrollably.

"Geez, what a coward!" Mesquite said, exasperated.

"Yeah," Sequoia chimed in, "I was hoping to do that for him – with my fist."

Juniper ran over to the crumpled villain to make sure he was still alive. Standing on his chest, she could tell he was still breathing. "Aw, crud!" she let out, "I was so looking forward to kicking his butt myself."

"You think he thought we were going to eat him alive?" Cedar jested.

Aspen landed gently next to the group. "Can you believe this guy?" she said in disgust. "He'd rather knock himself out than give us the chance to do it. This guy's a wimp without all his toys."

"And a chicken," Mesquite added.

Cedar couldn't resist an opening like that. "I bet that's what he'd taste like, too!" he joked.

That afternoon, a large group of Voyageurs National Park authorities poured into Colonel Shaka's campsite. They were responding to reports of explosions and smoke in the sky. They weren't expecting what they found.

Colonel Shaka, the once mighty hunter, was just sitting there; propped against the pile of broken Soldierjacks with his hands tied behind him by the remnants of his once-savage bullwhip.

He was conscious but incoherent, blubbering to himself in broken sentences lathered with uncontrollable spittle. The Colonel from South Africa was completely dislodged mentally and continued to blather to nobody in particular as he was loaded into an awaiting ambulance under police escort.

The law officers on scene deduced he was a poacher of the highest order. The tents, cages, equipment and personal armament scattered around his campsite was evidence enough to summon a variety of charges from possession of illegal weapons to reckless endangerment. The lack of identification and any sort of registration or park passes further fueled their case against him.

Colonel Shaka was taken to the nearest hospital, an hour away in International Falls, for treatment and further

observation. The doctors did the best they could for his injuries, but there was little they could do for his mind. The massive shock he had given himself had amplified as it traveled down the circuits tied into his brain from his artificial eye. The result was catastrophic to his mental stability.

He was impossible to identify. His fingerprints were cross-referenced in the police database but came up as non-existent. Even his dental records proved worthless. He was a mystery indeed. As law enforcement put together their case against him with a long list of federal offenses, the hospital staff struggled to recoup his intellect. It was as if most of his brain cells had been wiped clean. He barely had the motor skills to feed himself.

Realizing he was physically, if not mentally, fully capable, the nursing staff allowed him a small amount of mobility as long as an armed guard was nearby. Dressed in the largest hospital gown available, the once cunning soldier of the Axxes empire had been reduced to a slow-moving, slow-thinking hulking figure that could hardly function on his own.

He was still a very large man with an unknown past and the National Park Service, as well as the state of Minnesota, planned to charge him with everything they could. It was possible that he was faking his mental state or perhaps could snap out of it at any moment and escape from custody.

Hoping that some interaction with youngsters would bring him around, the hospital allowed him to wander down to the children's ward as long as he had police escort. They thought that the environment there might feel more comfortable to the towering African. Immersing him amongst the bright colors, crayons and cartoon characters could prove beneficial.

At first it seemed to work. Like a monstrous-sized kid, the large fish tank and all the picture books lying around enthralled Shaka. He even paused to pick up a couple of toys and coddled a bright yellow robot in his massive hands for a few minutes.

But then everything went wrong. The gentle giant without a name walked behind a small bookshelf to a play area that was set aside there. A cute round red table with cute little blue chairs around it was covered with an assortment of stuffed animals.

Without warning, the once tranquil patient freaked out. Staring at the toy animals, Colonel Shaka started screaming and thrashing about as he tried to retreat. He stumbled backwards, terrified of the fluffy critters with the big plastic eyes and large pink bows. Like a football player scrambling for a touchdown, he rushed out of the children's ward, tossing aside the policeman and any nurses who tried to slow his exit.

He was tackled by a couple of orderlies down the hall and sedated. They handcuffed him to his bed. He was

transported to jail that evening.

*****

Suddenly, Voyageurs National Park was a hotbed of activity. A local news station had aired an interview with a family that claimed their 12-year-old son had spotted a black lynx. The family then went on to tell their story about being harassed by a motorcycle gang that was then somehow overpowered while they were locked inside their cabin.

People, media outlets in particular, started pouring into the park. Word had gotten out.

At a ranger station in the northwest part of the park, several witnesses were shocked to see a large mother black lynx followed by two kittens brazenly walk right out in the open and seemingly pose for pictures. People scrambled for their cameras, capturing the threesome as they sat there basking in the sun.

Even the park ranger came out of his little shack to watch the newly discovered species as they slowly wandered back into the forest, seemingly waiting for them to follow. Captivated by the beautiful ebony-colored wildcats, the group, led by the park ranger himself, cautiously followed them deep into the woods.

Observing from as far back as possible, they trailed the black lynxes for nearly two miles until they came

across an old abandoned iron ore mine. The cats, clearly aware of the humans snapping photos and shooting video from their little handheld cameras, walked into the front doors of the mine which seemed to have been recently ripped open from the inside by something quite large and powerful.

The ranger convinced the horde of followers to stay back as he relayed the events back to his headquarters. Soon other park authorities arrived and, armed with flashlights, they went inside the Axxes-owned mine. After nearly an hour, they came out. They didn't find the black lynxes – the three wildcats had somehow escaped – but what they did find was far more shocking.

By the next day, the mine was crawling with police and federal officials. A delegation of armed Air Force personnel had arrived and the place was swarming with investigators, FBI and other government agencies.

Three black lynxes had seemingly uncovered the secret nuclear warhead stash of Nathan Axxes. He would be in court explaining, bribing, and lying his way out of federal prison for years to come.

*****

About a week later, Mesquite, Sequoia, Aspen, Cedar and Juniper were frolicking in the thick, wet grass of a quiet meadow just south of the park. They loved this

land. It was clean, lush and brimming with life. Water was everywhere and the trees offered millions of places to hide or seek shelter. It seemed like the perfect place to live – at least in the warmer months.

"I think we should just stay here," Cedar said as he gazed around at the glorious terrain. "Maybe our mission is done, maybe we can just be kids again. Right here. Forever."

"We all know that's just not going to happen," Mesquite said. "But I wish it were so."

"Yeah, m-m-me too," Sequoia added. "I've never had so m-m-much fish to eat in my whole life!"

"You guys, we can't ignore our life's purpose," Juniper said. She looked lovingly at the countryside, her heart wanted to do just as they did and settle forever near this pristine gigantic national park. But she knew a black-footed ferret wouldn't have much of an existence in northern Minnesota in the winter.

Aspen fluttered up and landed on an outstretched branch on a nearby birch tree. "We gotta keep moving," she said. "I think it's time we headed west."

"West?" Cedar asked. "Why west?"

"Oh, I just got a feeling," she said and then she used her wing to point to the sky. Above them, several clouds had pushed themselves together to form a gigantic arrow that clearly was pointing westerly. It was a supernatural sign that they just couldn't ignore.

"A few miles south of here, there's a train track that runs east and west," Aspen reported. "I say we hop an empty car on the next west-bound train and see where it takes us."

"Agreed," Mesquite said, but with little conviction. He had heard the wolf howls off in the distance the night before and he longed to be with his own kind. But he knew that could never be.

"What d-d-do you guys sup-sup-suppose happened to the hunter man?" Sequoia asked the group. "Do you guys th-th-think he'll ever hunt again?"

"Oh, I'm sure he's hunting right now," Cedar said with a coy smile. His four friends looked at him quizzically with furrowed brows. "Hunting for a way out of prison, that is!"

That got the group laughing again and they decided that just a few more precious moments in the Northwoods wilderness as best friends on life's greatest adventure was the greatest gift of all.

DAVID A. SCHMIDT
Artist & Author

BIO

Born and raised in rural Wisconsin, David Schmidt has always had an aptitude for artistic endeavors. Upon graduating with honors from high school, Schmidt moved to Colorado and joined the National Guard as a means to pursue an art degree.

After returning home from a deployment with his unit for Operation Desert Shield/Desert Storm in 1991, Schmidt worked for a Denver-based children's book fair-company. It was in those elementary schools and working with the kids, teachers and parents that he found himself drawn to creating his own children's books.

Meanwhile, Schmidt moved into a position for the Colorado National Guard as an illustrator, then military journalist and, finally, as historian. These occupations honed his skills and guided him further down his path toward publishing.

David Schmidt resides in Lone Tree, Colorado, with his wife and is the owner of Media Uprising - a creative company that serves as the outlet for his diverse talents. He holds a degree in Interactive Media Design from the Art Institute of Pittsburgh.